"More," Emily said sleepily. "I want to hear more."

Nicola read on, relating Charmaine's adventures, finishing with, "'I miss you, Nic. Whistler isn't the same without you. Lots of love, Charmaine.'"

Emily's soft breathing was even and her eyes had shut. Nicola folded the letter and tucked it back into the envelope. She missed Charmaine, too. Her cousin had been witty and warm and fun. She'd dragged Nicola to parties and dances, embarrassing ordeals for a shy wallflower like herself, but Charmaine always made sure some boy danced with her less popular cousin. If, in hindsight, her behavior seemed patronizing, Nicola knew Charmaine had meant well.

Nicola pulled the covers over her and Emily. In her sleep Emily wriggled closer. The girl's small body snuggled against her sent a rush of tenderness through Nicola.

Poor Charmaine. She'll never get to see her daughter grow up.

D0976342

Dear Reader,

I love Christmas! I love the freshness and purity of new-fallen snow and the excitement in a child's eyes at the sight of gaily wrapped presents piled below a lit Christmas tree. Spending time with family and friends, giving and sharing, rituals and traditions—these things give our lives meaning.

Christmas in Australia, where I now live, takes place in summer and is very different from what I was used to growing up in Canada. We've created new traditions, like a Christmas barbecue and an early-morning swim, but writing A *Mom for Christmas* was special because it allowed me to relive the kind of Christmas I knew as a child.

No matter were you live, true love can find you in your darkest hour. In A *Mom for Christmas* Aidan Wilde's wife, Charmaine, died on Christmas Eve under tragic and mysterious circumstances. Left alone to raise their baby daughter, Aidan lost his Christmas spirit until his late wife's cousin, Nicola Bond, brought a little Christmas magic into their lives.

A *Mom for Christmas* is the third and last book in my WILDE MEN trilogy, following *Homecoming Wife* and *Family Matters*. I bid a sad but fond farewell to Aidan, his brother, Nate, and their cousin Marc. I hope you've enjoyed reading about them as much as I've enjoyed writing their stories.

I love to hear from my readers. Please write to me at P.O. Box 234, Point Roberts, WA 98281-0234, or visit me online at www.joankilby.com and send an e-mail.

Sincerely,

Joan Kilby

Joan Kilby

A Mom for Christmas

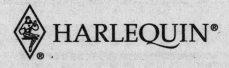

HARLEQUIN®

TORONTO • NEW YORK • LONDON
AMSTERDAM • PARIS • SYDNEY • HAMBURG
STOCKHOLM • ATHENS • TOKYO • MILAN • MADRID
PRAGUE • WARSAW • BUDAPEST • AUCKLAND

If you purchased this book without a cover you should be aware
that this book is stolen property. It was reported as "unsold and
destroyed" to the publisher, and neither the author nor the
publisher has received any payment for this "stripped book."

ISBN 0-373-71236-7

A MOM FOR CHRISTMAS

Copyright © 2004 by Joan Kilby.

All rights reserved. Except for use in any review, the reproduction or
utilization of this work in whole or in part in any form by any electronic,
mechanical or other means, now known or hereafter invented, including
xerography, photocopying and recording, or in any information storage
or retrieval system, is forbidden without the written permission of the
publisher, Harlequin Enterprises Limited, 225 Duncan Mill Road,
Don Mills, Ontario, Canada M3B 3K9.

All characters in this book have no existence outside the imagination of
the author and have no relation whatsoever to anyone bearing the same
name or names. They are not even distantly inspired by any individual
known or unknown to the author, and all incidents are pure invention.

This edition published by arrangement with Harlequin Books S.A.

® and TM are trademarks of the publisher. Trademarks indicated with
® are registered in the United States Patent and Trademark Office, the
Canadian Trade Marks Office and in other countries.

www.eHarlequin.com

Printed in U.S.A.

Gavin Reed of the Whistler-Blackcomb ski patrol
was of invaluable assistance in researching this book.
All errors are mine.

Don't miss any of our special offers. Write to us at the
following address for information on our newest releases.

Harlequin Reader Service
U.S.: 3010 Walden Ave., P.O. Box 1325, Buffalo, NY 14269
Canadian: P.O. Box 609, Fort Erie, Ont. L2A 5X3

CHAPTER ONE

AIDAN WILDE SCANNED the snowy slope, alert for skiers in trouble. Below the ridge, Whistler Mountain glowed silvery-blue in the fading light on this December afternoon. Every mogul, every half-submerged outcropping of granite was as familiar to Aidan as the swooshing of his skis through the crisp snow.

The eerie quality of the shadowed cliff face called forth memories of Charmaine. The place she'd fallen from was higher, in the permanently closed area near the peak, but as Aidan made his descent thoughts of his late wife skirted the edge of his mind. Six years on he could still see the look of surprise and horror in her eyes as she went over the precipice.

Lights winked on along the chairlift above him, dispelling the shadows and bringing his mind back to the present. Charmaine was gone. He'd failed her then and he could do nothing for her now, except take care of their daughter, Emily, who'd been a tiny baby when her mother had died. Keeping Emily safe, watching her grow up healthy and strong, was all that mattered.

A sudden gust of wind whipped the tops of the snowdrifts into a flurry of white. Aidan increased his speed, looking forward to picking up Emily from her grandmother's and going home to their log house on the shores of Alta Lake. He and Emily would eat beef stew slow-cooked in the Crock-Pot then sit in front of the fire and read fairy tales of beautiful princesses living in remote towers. With no one to disturb their tranquil happiness they could wear their happy faces and pretend all was right with the world.

Outside the alpine patrol hut Aidan removed his skis and put them into the ski rack. Stamping snow from his boots, he clumped inside the bump room where the men and women of the ski patrol congregated. Several patrollers were seated at wooden tables playing cards. Others, like his partner Frederik, had come in from patrol and were removing their outer wear at wooden benches around the room's perimeter.

"You are first on the mountain in the morning and last off in the evening," Frederik commented good-naturedly in his precise Swiss-German accent. With his shaved head and once-broken nose he could be intimidating to those who didn't know his gentle side.

Aidan shrugged out of the red-and-gray ski patrol jacket with the white cross on the back. "Just doing my job."

Truth was, he lived and breathed Whistler Mountain. He'd grown up in its protective shadow and as a man viewed the world from its soaring peak, first as a downhill racer and now in the ski patrol. If not for the grounding influence of Emily he might spend all his time up here.

"Aidan!" Rich Waller strode across the room, black Gore-Tex pants rustling. His thermal undershirt clung to a well-developed torso and his thinning blond hair was stuck to his scalp with perspiration. "Christy's looking for the incident report on the tourist with the broken leg you transported off the mountain this morning. Did you forget to log the information?"

Aidan glanced through the glass wall separating the bump room from the dispatcher's office. Christy, seeing him look her way, tucked a long blond strand of hair behind her ear and smiled. Aidan lifted a hand in greeting and turned back to Rich. "I didn't forget. I just got busy."

"Oh, okay." Rich shrugged. "I was in the dispatch office when the call came in so I started it for you."

"You didn't need to do that," Aidan said.

"I don't mind. No trouble at all." Rich smiled and walked off toward the coffee machine.

"Rich can be *too* helpful," Frederik said in a dry undertone.

Aidan sank onto the bench beside Frederik, pulled off his ski boots and wriggled his cramped toes in their thick wool socks. "He means well."

"But he makes you look bad when you haven't done anything wrong," Frederik persisted. "Why do you let him?"

"Rich and I go back a long way. He was my partner for years until…until my wife died. Afterward I took a couple of months off and when I came back we'd both been reassigned."

Rich had seen Charmaine come off the lift that tragic day on the mountain and he knew things no one else did about the circumstances surrounding her death. Aidan had walked on eggshells until Rich made it tacitly clear he wouldn't say anything to anyone, not even the police. Ski patrol was about teamwork, camaraderie and trust. Aidan couldn't fault Rich but somehow their relationship had never been quite the same, underscored as it was by subtle power plays on Rich's part and tolerance on Aidan's.

"He's jealous of you," Frederik said. "You're a better skier and more well-liked, especially with the ladies."

"Nah," Aidan scoffed. "It's true Rich used to go

out with my late wife until I came along, but he was over that long ago." Aidan was getting uncomfortable; time to change the subject. "Any word on your contract?"

Frederik's face lit as he swiveled on the bench to face Aidan. "It's been renewed for the winter season. Bob told me just before you came in," he added, referring to the assistant patrol manager. "Feel like a drink to celebrate?"

"Thanks, but not tonight." Aidan stood and peeled off his black ski pants. "Your girlfriend will be pleased you're staying on in Whistler."

"Liz is meeting me at Dusty's," Frederik said. "Come on, join us. I could ask her to bring a friend."

A couple of years after Charmaine's death, when the shock and grief had eased a little, Aidan had played the field, going out with a different woman every week. Gradually he'd lost interest in romances that went nowhere as he came to the sobering conclusion that after Charmaine, the chances of him forming a lasting relationship were slim to nil.

That hadn't stopped his brother, Nate; his cousin, Marc; and now Frederik, from inundating Aidan with unwelcome attempts at matchmaking. Maybe if he told them the real reason he wasn't looking to replace Charmaine they would accept he would always be a loner. But that was between him and the mountain.

"Emily's waiting for me and I've got paperwork to do before I leave," Aidan said. "Maybe another time."

"*Ja*, sure," Frederik said with cheerful skepticism. Rising, he gathered up his uniform and ski boots to carry them to his locker. "See you tomorrow."

Aidan finished changing and went to the dispatch office to file his report. Christy glanced up from her computer screen. "Hey, Aidan, how's it going?"

"Not bad. Rich said you were looking for the 10-40 on the woman with the broken leg."

Rolling her eyes, Christy handed him a half-finished form. "I only asked him if you were on your way in to base. I knew you'd file when you got a chance."

Aidan pulled a waterproof notebook from his pocket and, flipping to the correct page, began to transfer the information. The two-way radio crackled in the background and Christy turned her attention to taking the details of a call-in from another patroller. Aidan finished filling in the incident report and when Christy was free, handed it to her. Then he pulled on his gloves and lifted a hand in farewell. "Catch you later."

"Wait, Aidan." Christy rose and leaned over the counter, her fingers playing with the end of her ponytail. "Are you going to Dusty's?"

"Not tonight. I've got to get home to Emily,"

Aidan said quickly and smoothly. Christy was a good friend and he wanted to keep it that way.

Her full mouth curved downward in a disappointed droop. "You're no fun."

"A gorgeous girl like you will find someone to play with." Aidan smiled warmly to take the sting out of his refusal. "Catch you later."

He caught the gondola down the mountain and made his way through the village to his Land Cruiser, his boots crunching on the icy crusts of snow left by the plow. The streetlights came on as he drove out of Whistler Village and down Highway 99 to Emerald Estates where Charmaine's mother, June, lived with her husband Roy in a two-story timber home among towering hemlock and spruce trees.

June cared for Emily after school and on Saturdays when Aidan's shift fell on the weekend. Although she never came right out and accused him, he knew his mother-in-law blamed him for Charmaine's death; certainly she didn't believe his eyewitness account of her daughter's last minutes alive.

Aidan drove through the gathering dark, picturing Emily waiting for him as she did every night, her small nose pressed against the window as she peered into the winter gloom, looking for the lights of his vehicle to turn into the driveway. Maybe Marc and Nate were right, he did need to get a life, but at the end of the day he didn't care about anything very much as long as he had Emily.

NICOLA BOND STEPPED OFF THE BUS at the Village Gate Boulevard, her stainless-steel camera case in hand and another camera bag slung over her shoulder. After the heat and humidity of Sydney the crisp mountain air bit her cheeks and sent her digging in the pockets of her navy down jacket for her gloves. A snowflake melted on her nose and she glanced up at the darkening sky to see fluffy white flecks drifting in the glow of the streetlight.

Instantly she was transported back to her childhood in Whistler before her family moved to Australia. She and her cousin Charmaine had gone skiing and ice-skating together, then as they'd grown older, Charmaine had taken Nicola to parties and dances. Charmaine had been beautiful, funny and smart. Everyone, including Nicola, had loved her.

"This your bag, miss?" The driver hauled her battered blue suitcase from the storage compartment beneath the bus and placed it on the hard-packed snow.

"Thanks." Nicola's breath came out in little puffs of condensation. With all her luggage accounted for she headed for a nearby phone booth.

She dialed her aunt's number and glanced at her

watch. Only four-thirty and it was already dark; she'd forgotten the early winter nights in Canada.

"June Greene speaking," a cultured feminine voice said.

In the background Nicola could hear a high-pitched child's voice. With a surge of excitement she wondered if she was listening to Charmaine's little girl.

"Aunt June? It's me, Nic."

"Nicola!" her aunt exclaimed with pleasure. "Where *are* you?"

"In Whistler. I just arrived on the bus."

June made a sound of exasperation. "You should have told us which flight you were coming in on. We'd have met you at the airport."

"I didn't want to put you out. The bus was fine. I'm calling now to let you know I'm here, instead of just turning up on your doorstep."

"Roy is still at work and I'm stuck here at the house until Aidan picks up Emily," June said. "If you want to find a place to have a coffee I'll come for you as soon as he leaves."

Aidan. Nicola had a crush on him in high school, a hopeless infatuation which she'd never even confided to Charmaine. Years later, when her cousin wrote that she was going to marry him, Nicola had thrust her jealousy aside; she could never compete with Charmaine.

She'd flown back to be a bridesmaid at Charmaine's wedding. Aidan was the dashing groom sweeping his beautiful bride into a fairy tale life, and so handsome he made Nicola's heart ache. That memory was in stark contrast to the snapshot June sent after Charmaine's funeral of a grief-ravaged widower at a snowy graveside, holding his baby daughter.

Adjusting her eyes to the outside she could see the snowflakes were falling thicker and faster. "No, please don't trouble yourself. I'll get a taxi."

She walked back to the Yellow Cab waiting at the taxi stand next to the bus stop and gave the driver her aunt's address in Emerald Estates. Nicola burrowed into the corner of the back seat and peered through the window as the taxi bore her away. The tires sounded muffled on the thin layer of freshly fallen snow as they drove past expensive new condominiums and town houses. The resort had grown almost beyond recognition since she'd lived here, but the towering peaks of Whistler and Blackcomb Mountains that guarded the valley were comfortingly familiar.

June opened the door before Nicola could ring the bell. Her blond hair shining above a black cashmere cardigan, she opened her arms and enveloped Nicola in a warm embrace and a cloud of expensive perfume. "I can't believe you're here at last. You *are* staying for Christmas, aren't you? Your father didn't seem to know when I talked to him. He said something about a photography assignment."

"That's right," Nicola said. "I'm meeting a colleague, a travel writer, here in January. I'm sorry it's so last-minute but we just got the go-ahead on the book. I came early so I could spend the holiday with you and Uncle Roy."

"That's what I was hoping," June said, releasing her. "When I heard you were coming I wrote my mother in Edmonton and asked her if she could get out to the coast, too."

"I'd love to see Grammy." Nicola let her camera case slide to floor. "Is she going to make it?"

"The last I heard she was trying to get a flight. Let's not stand around in the hall. Give me that wet coat and come into the living room. Boots off, too, please—the carpets, you know. Aidan isn't here yet so you're in time to meet Emily." June helped her out of her damp jacket, and hung it on the newel post at the base of the staircase.

As June spoke, Nicola caught a glimpse of a small blond head peeking around the door frame behind her aunt's back. No sooner did Nicola meet the girl's shy blue gaze than she ducked out of sight.

Nicola levered her feet out of her hiking boots and followed June into the elegant and formal living room, eager to get to know the little girl she'd thought about so often over the years. June had sent photos of Emily to Nicola's mother every Christmas, but without Charmaine's chatty letters Nicola knew few details about the girl. Nicola had written to Aidan after the funeral to express her condolences, but he'd never answered her letter and she hadn't pursued further correspondence.

"Emily," June called, glancing around. A toy tea set laid for two had been abandoned near the base of an artificial Christmas tree with silver needles and red ornaments. "Your cousin Nicola's here from Australia. Come out and say hello like a good girl." June met Nicola's gaze apologetically, explaining in an undertone, "She's bashful at first but once she gets to know you, she's very charming, just like her mother." Speaking louder, she tried to coax Emily, "We're not playing hide-and-seek now, sweetheart."

"Leave her," Nicola begged, knowing firsthand how painful it was to be shy. "She'll come out when she's ready."

"I suppose so," June said. "If only her father would encourage her to be more social instead of hiding away with her like a hermit."

Nicola was surprised at her aunt's disapproving tone. She nodded to the sofa where the girl crouched out of sight. "Is there a problem?"

"Not with *her*. It's *him*. I won't go into it now. Little pitchers have big ears, if you know what I mean." She gestured to the antique sofa. "Sit down and tell me all about your work. I must say, you haven't changed. You look exactly the same as the day you left Whistler."

Considering Nicola had been fifteen when she'd left and was now twenty-seven she wasn't sure her aunt's assessment was entirely complimentary even if it was largely accurate. She had the same chin-length blunt cut brown hair and the same waifish figure clad in bulky clothes of neutral shades that tended to blend in with her surroundings. Not that she was exactly color-coordinated with the pale-pink brocade covering June's sofa.

In a few words she related the highlights of her career so far; taking photos of children with Santa Claus, graduating to studio portrait work, evolving to calendars and tourism assignments and finally culminating in her present job, freelance travel photography.

As she spoke she could hear faint scuffling sounds coming from behind the sofa where Emily was hiding. June went out of the room after murmuring something about coffee and Nicola was tempted to peek over the back to say hello. Instead she waited to see what Emily would do. The girl didn't emerge.

Before long June returned with a tray bearing a pair of bone china coffee cups. Nicola glanced around for something to protect the polished surface of the pie-crust table at her elbow. She'd forgotten how intimidating her aunt's home could be for someone used to putting her stocking feet up on the furniture and eating her dinner off her lap in front of the TV.

June supplied her with a coaster and sat beside her. "Tell me more about this book you're working on."

"Reiner's been commissioned to do a coffee-table book on the ski resorts of Canada and the United States. He's asked me to take the photos. It's a fantastic opportunity professionally, plus I get to travel, visit my family and ski all the best mountains in North America." Nicola paused to sip her coffee. "I haven't done much skiing since moving to Australia and I miss it. Charmaine and I used to spend all our spare time on the mountain when we were girls."

June's face tightened, her smile freezing. "I remember."

"I'm sorry," Nicola murmured, kicking herself for referring to her cousin in the context of Whistler Mountain. "Her loss must still be painful for you."

"It always will be." The awkward silence was broken by the sound of a car turning into the driveway. June exhaled in relief and rose to go out to the hall. "That will be Aidan. Don't worry, he won't stay long."

Emily popped up from behind the sofa and pressed her nose to the window, her small hands shielding her eyes to peer into the darkness. Her entire attention was on her father's arrival, as if she'd been waiting for this moment the whole day. Nicola thought she seemed small for her age, more like a four- or five-year-old than a child of six. Odd, since Charmaine had been tall and Aidan was at least six foot two. Before Nicola could say hello Emily squeezed out from behind the sofa and in a blur of pink wool and purple corduroy, ran to the front door.

Nicola listened to June's brisk report to Aidan about Emily's day—what she ate for lunch and how much TV she'd watched after school. Aidan replied in curt phrases interspersed with instructions to Emily to get her snowsuit and boots. Clearly he was as impatient to be gone as June was to have him leave.

Nicola stayed where she was. She was disappointed at not getting a chance to talk to Emily but she didn't particularly care if she met Aidan. She'd gotten over her crush a long time ago. At Charmaine's wedding he'd looked right through her; chances were he'd do the same now. Attractive men like Aidan tended to treat her as if she were invisible.

"Wait, Daddy! I've got to get the tea set Grandma

gave me." Emily raced around the corner into the living room. Throwing Nicola a swift glance she knelt on the carpet to gather up the child-size china cups and saucers.

"Another present?" Aidan, sounding exasperated, said to June. "It's not Christmas yet."

"I saw it in the store and knew Emily would love it," June replied. "Don't spoil my fun."

Nicola had to strain to hear Aidan's next words. "I wish *you* wouldn't spoil *her*."

Then unexpectedly, Aidan stood in the open double doorway, his athletic frame topped by windblown chestnut hair and searching green eyes. Despite her claim to indifference Nicola found her attention caught.

Aidan's gaze skimmed over the sofa where she sat and came to rest on his daughter. "Hurry, Em. Let's get going."

Generally Nicola ignored such minor snubs but something made her stand and force him to notice her. "Hi, I'm Nicola."

"Nic is Emily's second cousin," June explained coming into the room. "My brother Stan's daughter from Australia. She's in town to take pictures of the ski resort."

Aidan's face changed, registering recognition if not interest. "You were in the wedding party."

So he *had* noticed her. Amazing. "I was maid of honor."

Emily tugged on his pant leg. "Can we go now, Daddy?"

"I'll get her backpack," June said and left.

"Did you say hello to Nicola?" Aidan asked Emily.

Emily glanced shyly up at Nicola and whispered, "Hi."

Nicola dropped to a crouch. The little girl looked astonishingly like Charmaine, with glowing pink skin and huge blue eyes. "Hi, Emily. Your mommy wasn't just my cousin, she was my best friend. She was a year older than me and we shared everything, just as if we were sisters. She wrote me lots of letters and I brought them with me because I thought you might like to hear what she had to say."

Emily buried her face in her dad's jacket.

Aidan lifted his daughter's chin. "Remember what I said about putting on a happy face?" he said. She nodded and gave Nicola a brief, forced smile. "Good girl. Now finish packing up your tea set."

Emily ran back to her tea set and resumed placing the cups and plates into the box so carefully they barely made a sound.

Nicola turned to Aidan. "I never got a chance to say so in person but..." She lowered her voice out of respect. "I'm sorry about Charmaine."

"Thank you." His clipped response discouraged further conversation but she thought his gaze softened a little.

The two of them waited awkwardly, watching Emily. Nicola shoved her hands into the back pockets of her pants, tongue-tied. Aidan wasn't helping in the least; he looked as though his thoughts were a million miles away.

June's footsteps approached and Nicola turned with relief, only to groan inwardly when the phone rang in the kitchen and her aunt's steps changed direction.

Emily finished packing up. Aidan stooped to pick up the box. "Go get your snowsuit on."

Emily skipped out to the hall. Nicola trailed after. The girl climbed into her one-piece snowsuit then sat on the floor and struggled to get her foot into a boot.

"Where did those boots come from, Em?" her father said as he came through the doorway with the box under his arm.

"Grandma gave them to me. She said my old boots were ugly and she threw them away." The new boots had fake fur around the top and a zipper up the inside which Emily hadn't noticed. She was getting more baffled and defeated by the second.

Aidan muttered something about "too much," then said, "Pull the zipper down first."

Emily tried once and failed. "I can't."

"Try again," Aidan urged.

"I'm sorry I took so long." June appeared and handed Aidan a small bright pink backpack. Noticing Emily tugging at the zipper she kneeled and un-zipped it for her.

"You should let her do it herself, Aunt June," Nicola said, sympathizing with Aidan's evident frustration.

June rose and folded her hands at her waist, smiling genially. "I'm sure when you have children of your own you'll do a marvelous job, but I know my granddaughter." She turned to Aidan. "Candace Taylor called to ask if I'd help on the Christmas Ball committee. I had to tell her no, of course, because I look after my granddaughter during the day."

"I suppose I could make other arrangements for Emily," Aidan began slowly.

"I've got free time while I'm here," Nicola interrupted. "I'd be more than happy to look after her."

"No, dear, that's out of the question," June replied. "We can't rope you into baby-sitting during your visit."

"I don't mind, honest," Nicola countered. "Aidan, what do *you* think?"

CHAPTER TWO

AIDAN GLANCED OVER Nicola, really seeing her for the first time. She seemed an unlikely best friend for Charmaine, who would have outshone her younger cousin by a million watts. He would never have remembered Nicola except that she was in the wedding photo on his bedroom wall. However, she looked sensible, responsible and not in the least frivolous— the perfect antidote to his mother-in-law as caretaker for his overindulged daughter.

Besides, Nicola had been very close to Charmaine—who would be more fitting to care for Emily?

"I think it's a good idea," he said. "I appreciate your offer."

"She's here on business. She won't have time," June protested, clearly upset at being replaced so easily.

"I don't start work until after New Year's," Nicola insisted, her husky voice betraying a faint Australian accent. "Go ahead and join the committee, Aunt June. I know how much you enjoy getting your finger stuck into the community pie."

"You could use a break from baby-sitting, June," Aidan added. *And Emily needed a break from being spoiled rotten.* At times he was tempted to put his daughter in day care but June was still the child's grandmother and, though she could barely conceal her dislike of *him,* there was no doubt she adored Emily. "I insist."

"Well, if you put it like that," June said stiffly. "Thank you, Nicola, for your help. I do enjoy working on the Christmas Ball."

As June left the room to call her friend back Aidan felt compelled to warn Nicola, "Emily may look like Charmaine but she isn't as outgoing as her mother. She doesn't take to newcomers readily."

Nicola brushed off his warning with a skeptical lift of one olive-drab shoulder. "She's just a little shy. We'll be friends in no time."

Part of him wanted badly to believe that. For years they'd been a unit, complete within themselves. Now that Emily was going to school he'd begun to realize she needed other people, even if he didn't.

"I usually bring Emily over before I go to work in the morning then pick her up here after school," Aidan explained.

"What if I took her home to your house after school, instead?" she suggested. "That way she wouldn't have such a long day."

"Even better. I'll see you tomorrow morning at five-thirty." He smiled wryly as Nicola's eyebrows shot into her bangs. "I'm on avalanche control."

BENEATH EMILY'S snowsuit she wore one-piece pajamas the color of bubble gum with feet and a hood. She looked like a little pink cat without the whiskers.

"Be very quiet," Nicola said as they tiptoed up the stairs to the second-floor bedrooms. "Aunt June and Uncle Roy are still sleeping."

Emily made a motion as if zipping her lips. Nicola smiled; the child couldn't be too loud if she tried. Nicola paused beside a shut door to the left of the landing. "That was your mom's room when she was a girl. Maybe you can sleep in there until it's time to get up for school."

Emily's blue eyes widened as she shook her head vigorously. "I'm not allowed to go in there."

"Oh." Probably June had made it into a sewing room or something, with objects she didn't want disturbed by small sticky hands. Nicola turned to the right and opened the door to her room. "In that case you can crawl into bed with me."

The dresser was cluttered with cameras, film containers and lenses. Her suitcase was open on the chair beside the queen-size bed, her clothes spilling out. Hastily she gathered them up and stuffed them back in, flipping the lid shut.

Emily dutifully got under the covers and lay back on the pillow. "I'm not sleepy," she whispered in a lisp.

"You can talk in a normal voice now," Nicola told her with an encouraging smile. "I don't think Aunt June and Uncle Roy can hear you through these thick walls."

"I am talking normal," Emily said, barely audible.

"I see." Nicola paused. "Do you ever talk louder? Or laugh?"

Emily shook her head and regarded Nicola with a puzzled expression. "Why?"

"Just for fun. Because it makes you feel good."

"Like putting on a happy face?"

"Hmm, maybe. Show me your happy face."

Emily scrunched up her eyes and bared her gums, revealing the absence of her two front teeth.

Nicola laughed and gave her a hug. "Snuggle down and keep warm. I'll read to you."

Nicola pulled a sheaf of old envelopes from the pocket of her suitcase then crawled into bed and puffed up the pillows. She chose a letter at random and adjusted the table lamp so it shone on the thin blue airmail paper. "This is a letter your mom wrote to me, let's see, eight years ago. She used to tell me all about her life and what she was doing. I saved all of her letters because they reminded me of her and of home. Your dad's in here, too.

"Dear Nic," she began. *"We had a blizzard yesterday and we're snowed in. I was afraid it would be days before I saw Aidan again but he skied over to the house. He looked so handsome with the snow in his hair...."*

Nicola recalled him on the doorstep this morning, thick snowflakes falling on his green knitted hat, melting in his black eyelashes. Briefly she tried to imagine Aidan skiing miles in a blizzard just to see her. Huh. As if *that* would ever happen.

"He asked me to go to the Christmas Ball just as I knew he would. Your mom had a lot of confidence when it came to guys," Nicola said in an aside to Emily and gave a small wistful sigh for her own lack of it. *"Last weekend I bought a new dress—red and slinky with a rhinestone circle in the center front and cut so low you can almost see my—* Ahem!" Nicola broke off. "Your mom was the most beautiful girl in all of Whistler and that dress...wow!"

Emily's eyes were aglow. "Did she look like a fairy princess?"

"Absolutely." A sexy young princess intent on

making her Prince Charming lose his mind, Nicola thought dryly. Which Aidan had, according to the juicy bits Nicola wasn't going to read aloud. She skipped ahead, past the ball, to a ski trip up Whistler Mountain. *"Today Aidan and I skied from The Cirque down the Glacier Bowl to Camel Back then all the way down the mountain on McConkey's."*

Nicola fell silent, thinking about the sketchy account she'd been given about Charmaine's death. Those trails were all advanced runs for expert skiers which made her cousin's fall all the more difficult to understand.

"More," Emily said sleepily. "I want to hear more."

Nicola read on, relating Charmaine's adventures both on the mountain and après skiing, finishing, *"I miss you, Nic. Whistler isn't the same without you. Lots of love, Charmaine."*

Emily's soft breathing was even and her eyes had fallen shut. Nicola folded the letter and tucked it back in the envelope, recalling the old days in Whistler. Her cousin had dragged Nicola to parties and dances, embarrassing ordeals for a wallflower like herself, but Charmaine always made sure some boy danced with her less popular cousin. If in hindsight her behavior seemed patronizing Nicola knew she'd meant well.

Nicola pulled the covers over her and Emily,

checked that the alarm was set and turned out the light. In her sleep Emily wriggled closer. The girl's small body snuggled against her sent a rush of tenderness through Nicola.

Poor Charmaine, never getting to see her daughter grow up.

AIDAN MOVED CAREFULLY across the dark windswept ridge near Whistler's peak, testing the stability of a fresh fall of snow with his ski pole. He and Frederik had come up the mountain on snowmobiles before dawn. Four inches of snow had fallen overnight, creating the possibility of the top layer sliding over the one beneath and starting an avalanche.

Aidan jammed his pole deep into the snow. The top layer shifted a couple of inches and stopped. He watched it a moment more then sidestepped up the slope, moving on.

Down in the valley half an hour earlier, the blurry lights of the snowplows had been traveling slowly up the highway when Aidan, half asleep, bundled Emily into the Land Cruiser. Side roads were blank white rivers and the branches of the trees lining them were weighed down with thick white clumps. At the entrance to Emerald Estates they'd gotten out at the bottom of the hill and walked up the unplowed road to June's house where a light burned over the snow-blanketed porch.

Nicola, shivering at the gust of chill air, opened the door to his knock in a thick terry-towel robe that dwarfed her slight figure. Her smile had warmed the frigid predawn in a welcome for Emily and his daughter had readily taken her hand after hugging him goodbye.

Here on the peak, all was cold and dark. Close by, Frederik prodded another section of the ridge, working his way toward Aidan. They always operated in pairs, keeping a sharp eye out for each other. Over on Blackcomb Mountain he could hear a series of muffled booms as other members of the avalanche team "shot" the slope with sticks of an explosive emulsion.

White breath wreathing around his head, Frederik trudged across the ridge line toward him. "What do you think? Seems a little unstable to me."

"A few sections are marginal," Aidan agreed. "We'll ski-cut it."

Pink tinged the sky as Aidan made the first adrenaline-charged crossing of the pristine slope to trigger a small avalanche of the unstable surface layer. The low rumbling tremor of sliding snow made him glance over his shoulder. Balls of snow the size of small boulders tumbled down the mountain behind him. Seconds ahead of the slide, he whooshed to safety on the far side of the bowl. He lifted a hand to Frederik, giving his partner the all-clear signal. Every day Aidan took calculated risks, requiring him to think on his feet; it's what kept the job interesting.

And a good thing, too, since he took absolutely no risks in his personal life.

By the time Aidan was making his last run the sun had risen above the mountain, turning Whistler Bowl into a glittering crystal goblet. He and Frederik returned to the bump room where the rest of the patrol was arriving for duty. The assistant patrol manager, Bob, a fit-looking fifty-year-old, briefed them on snow conditions then broke the patrollers into groups and assigned them zones. They were to ski the runs, checking for problems and fixing them before the lifts started operating.

Bob paused and a few people began to stir, thinking he was finished. Then he held up a hand. "I have an announcement. You're all aware I was on sick leave last month. What you may not know is the reason. I suffered a minor heart attack."

He was forced to pause while people turned to each other with expressions of shock and disbelief. When the noise died down, Bob continued. "I've been doing a lot of thinking since then, weighing up my options. I've decided to take early retirement, as of the new year." Again, Bob had to hold up his hands to quell the clamor. "Anyone interested in my job is invited to submit an application to Human Resources. Now, let's get out on the mountain before the skiers arrive."

Everyone stood where they were, still stunned by the turn of events until Aidan drew on his hat and gloves and headed for the door. Then, in a swish of Gore-Tex and clumping of ski boots on wood, the ski patrollers shuffled out of the bump room.

"Aidan." Rich's voice brought Aidan to a halt.

Aidan signaled to Frederik to go ahead. "Hey, Rich. What's up?"

"I can't believe Bob's retiring," Rich said. "How could he have a heart attack? He's so healthy."

"I gather heart problems run in his family," Aidan said. "We're losing a friend as well as a great boss."

Rich pulled on his gloves and took out the knitted hat stuffed in his pocket. "Will you apply for the job?"

"Probably," Aidan said. "And you?"

"Of course. It's a great opportunity." He paused and squinted sideways at Aidan. "You don't think… nah, never mind."

"What?" Aidan glanced through the open door to where Frederik was waiting.

"I just wondered if management would give you a hard time over what happened, you know, with Charmaine."

"That was a long time ago," Aidan protested. But the mere reminder started a gnawing feeling in his stomach.

"You're right. Forget I mentioned it." Rich tugged his hat over his head and clapped Aidan on the shoulder. "Catch you later, buddy."

He strode off, leaving Aidan in turmoil. Would the Whistler Mountain management team have forgotten, or at least forgiven, the cloud that surrounded him over what happened six years ago? Now that Emily was old enough to understand the rumors that still circulated about him, the last thing he wanted was for the circumstances of Charmaine's death to be raked up again.

Frederik was waiting for Aidan outside by the ski rack. He took one look at Aidan's face and said, "Something is wrong, *ja?*"

Aidan put on his mirrored sunglasses. He literally trusted Frederik with his life, he had to in this job, but he couldn't bring himself to confide in him. "I was just thinking about Emily."

Frederik slid his skis out of the rack and dropped them to the ground to lock his boots into the bindings. "You worry about your daughter too much.

Relax. Whatever is the problem, everything will be okay," he advised. "Kids are tougher than you think."

For Emily's sake, Aidan hoped he was right.

NICOLA GOT BEHIND THE WHEEL of June's Suburban and familiarized herself with the controls. Emily was sitting in the back, blond hair braided and tucked under her bright multicolored hat. June sat in the front passenger seat and clasped her gloved hands tightly together as if to stop herself from reaching over and taking control of the car.

"Are you sure you know how to drive on the right side of the road?" June asked nervously. "It's not like Australia."

"No problem," Nicola replied breezily. Her aunt had arranged a ride home with a neighbor, leaving Nicola use of the vehicle; and Nicola refused to be stuck home simply because she'd learned to drive on the left-hand side of the road. The snow-packed streets added an unexpected challenge, but she'd bluffed her way through more difficult situations than this.

"Well, okay," June said doubtfully. "Turn right when you get to the highway."

"I know." Nicola turned off the radio, the better to concentrate, and backed out of the driveway. Emerald Drive had been plowed while they were having breakfast but was nevertheless more like one wide lane than two. She pointed the vehicle downhill. So far so good.

Once they were on the highway it was easier; she could follow other cars. She dropped June off at the Whistler Conference Center for her committee meeting before taking Emily on to Myrtle Philip Elementary.

"My other grandmother lives there," Emily said, pointing down the road toward the Tapley Estate.

Nicola remembered attending a prewedding dinner at Aidan's parents' house in one of the older subdivisions in Whistler. His father's business was building log homes and his mother was a public health nurse. Aidan had two brothers—no, one brother and a cousin who had grown up with them. She remembered being overawed by the three handsome athletic young men.

Cars were lined up along the school road for parents to drop their children off. Nicola maneuvered the big vehicle into a vacated slot and parked. Snowballs flew in the playground and some of the children were sliding down a small hill on plastic disks.

Nicola took Emily's hand and walked up the scraped and salted paved walk to the front doors of the school. "Your grandmother called to tell the principal I'd be picking you up," she explained to the girl.

"I'll come in and introduce myself to your teacher so she knows who I am."

"I'll take you to my classroom," Emily said importantly. "You can see my picture of a snowman."

As they entered the building a striking blond woman came out. Her bright red hat and tailored winter coat trimmed with black fur matched the color of her lips. She wore black leather gloves and leather fashion boots.

"Hi, Emily." She smiled at the girl and eyed Nicola with friendly curiosity. She hesitated as if she would have stopped to talk, but Emily tugged on Nicola's hand, leading her into the school.

"Who was that?" Nicola glanced over her shoulder to see the other woman also looking back.

"My auntie Angela."

"Is she married to your dad's brother?" Nicola guessed.

Emily nodded. "Uncle Nate."

"Do her kids go to school here, too?"

"She doesn't have any kids, but sometimes she drops off Ricky. He's in grade six. She's his aunt, too, but he's not my cousin." Emily gave a puzzled sigh. "Grandma explained it but I don't really understand."

Nicola was still trying to work out the family tree when Emily stopped in front of a classroom. The walls were covered with wobbly snowmen with black pipes and bowler hats and folded paper cutout snowflakes. "That's mine," Emily said, pointing to one of the drawings.

"It's very good," Nicola commended. "After school we can build a snowman in the backyard."

Nicola glanced through the open door. An older woman dressed in black pants and a red and green sweater with a Christmas motif was seated at a desk at the front of the room, marking papers. She looked vaguely familiar. "What's your teacher's name?"

"Mrs. Winston."

"Mrs. Winston?" Nicola laughed in surprise. "She was *my* teacher in Squamish, before they had schools in Whistler." Although the older woman's hair was now gray, she wore it in the same smooth page-boy style as she had years ago. Nicola knocked on the door to announce her presence.

Mrs. Winston glanced up and asked politely, "May I help you?" Then she noticed Emily. "Good morning, Emily. Is this your cousin who's looking after you for a while?"

"Second cousin, actually," Nicola said coming into the room. "I'm Nicola Bond. You probably don't remember me. I was in your grade five class back in—oh, I can't remember the year. Emily's mother, Charmaine, was my cousin."

Mrs. Winston rose and came forward, hand outstretched. "Nicola! I remember all my students. You were a quiet thing but you had such neat handwriting. I thought your family moved to Australia."

"That's right, Mrs. Winston. My parents bought a small farm outside Sydney. I'm here for work and to visit my aunt and uncle."

"Please, call me Sara," she said, smiling. "Is this the first time you've been back?"

"I was a bridesmaid at Charmaine's wedding." Her smile faded and she cast a quick glance toward Emily. The girl had gone to her desk midway down the far row. "I didn't get back for her funeral."

Sara shook her head and commiserated in a low voice. "A terrible tragedy. Poor Emily, only a baby. And the way Aidan's been pilloried by the community."

"What do you mean?" Nicola asked. "Why would he be pilloried?"

Sara frowned, as if suddenly realizing she'd said too much, and went back to her desk. "Nothing. It was just mean-spirited gossip."

"Gossip about what?" Nicola persisted.

"I shouldn't have said anything," Sara replied, shifting a pile of her students' printing exercises to one side. "I thought you'd know all about it since you're part of the family."

"My father and June are brother and sister but

they've never been particularly close. The most they communicate is a card and a family photo at Christmas."

"You should talk to your aunt," Sara told her. "It's not my place to say anything."

"June isn't comfortable talking about Charmaine." Nicola put a hand on her teacher's arm. "I'm probably going to run into this again and I have to deal with Emily's father. Please tell me what's going on."

"Well, all right," Sara said but with obvious reluctance. "It's not as though it's a secret. Everyone in Whistler talked about your cousin's death for years afterward. The case still divides the town. The coroner's inquest came back with a finding of death by misadventure. But although some people swear he's innocent, others are equally certain that…well, her death was no accident."

Nicola stared at the woman, hoping she wasn't hearing correctly. "You mean," she said carefully, "Aidan had something to do with Charmaine's death?"

Sara Winston's worried gaze met Nicola's scrutiny and she chewed her lip. "Aidan is a wonderful father and a supportive member of the school community. He—"

Her next words were cut off by the ringing of the

school bell. "I'm sorry," Sara said, rising. "You'll have to excuse me. The children will be coming in any second."

A door banged open down the hall and suddenly the air was filled with chattering, laughing kids and the drumming of booted feet on linoleum.

Nicola moved closer to be heard above the noise. "If Charmaine's fall from the mountain wasn't an accident—"

"Some say she was *pushed*," Sara whispered.

Nicola felt the blood drain from her cheeks. Her ears rang with echoes of the school bell. "Who would do such a thing?"

Long seconds passed while Sara Winston hesitated, clearly wishing she'd never started this conversation. At last she said, "Aidan was the only one there."

CHAPTER THREE

NICOLA HAD NO CHANCE to respond to the implied accusation. Children, red-cheeked and damp with snow, were pouring into the classroom, shrieking with high spirits.

"I'm afraid you'll have to go," Sara said above the din. "It was nice to see you again."

"Thanks for filling me in." *I think.*

Nicola waved goodbye to Emily who was already surrounded by her friends and pushed her way through the surge of grade ones. Sara's shocking declaration rang in her ears louder than the metallic clang of the school bell. *Charmaine's fall was no accident.*

That made Aidan a murderer.

Nicola stepped outside onto the concrete steps and shivered violently as the freezing air and the implication of Sara's words hit her simultaneously.

No, she thought in a violent rejection of the very idea. Aidan had been deeply in love with

Charmaine and she, with him. They had a brand-new baby and a bright future. Why would he kill her?

Nicola continued on her way back to the truck. Gossip was rife in the aftermath of dramatic events. People said all sorts of things without any evidence just to make life seem more interesting. Charmaine's letters were a testament to Aidan's devotion; proof of his adoration abounded in every line.

Still deep in thought Nicola started the engine and pulled out onto the road. A horn blared and she snapped into alertness to see a car coming straight at her. She swerved to the right at the last second and June's big vehicle fishtailed across the road, coming to rest with the front wheels embedded in a barrier of plowed snow.

"Stay on your own side of the road!" yelled the man in the red sedan whose car she'd almost hit head-on. He blasted his horn again as he went past.

Shaken, Nicola leaned on the steering wheel, bent head resting on her arms while her heart pounded furiously. She had to be more careful.

A rapping at her window made her lift her head. The blond woman, Emily's aunt Angela, was outside, peering in anxiously. Nicola rolled down the window.

"Are you all right?" Angela said. "That guy was a jerk."

"I *was* on the wrong side of the road," Nicola admitted. "But thanks."

"I'm Angela, Emily's aunt. Forgive me if I'm being nosy, but are you a friend of Aidan's?"

Nicola smiled. "Not exactly. I'm Nicola. Emily's mom, Charmaine, was my cousin and best friend when we were younger. I'm staying with my aunt for a while and offered to look after Emily while June helps on some committee."

During this speech Angela's bright blue eyes had widened. "I know who you are. You're the one who went to Australia." She glanced over her shoulder at a car trying to get past. "You're sticking out onto the road so we'd better not stand here yakking. How about getting together sometime soon? We never see much of Emily's other family."

"That'd be nice. What do you suggest?"

"Come for dinner tomorrow. Say, seven o'clock." Angela pulled out a card from her purse. "Here's the address."

"Thanks. I'll see you then."

Angela waved goodbye and picked her way through the clods of snow to her car. Nicola checked the rearview mirror and put the Suburban into Reverse. Its wheels spun, emitting a high-pitched whine. She shifted into four-wheel drive and tried again. The wheels caught and she backed jerkily onto the road. Chanting *keep to the right, keep to the right* under her breath, Nicola shifted into Drive and headed into Whistler.

She spent the day browsing the shops and taking photos of the picturesque village with its pedestrian-only streets decked out in pre-Christmas splendor. Later that afternoon she picked up Emily from school without mishap and drove south of Whistler, a short distance to Aidan's single-story log house on the shores of Alta Lake.

Nicola put the key Aidan had given her in the lock and opened the door to inviting smells of savory cooking, cedar and a wood fire. She hung her coat on a hook by the door and helped Emily out of her boots and snowsuit then followed the little girl to the great room whose high, wide windows overlooked the frozen lake.

Separating the living and dining areas was a large aquarium filled with colorful tropical fish. Facing the windows on the opposite wall was built-in shelving containing a TV, books and skiing trophies. A stone fireplace with an airtight insert was surrounded by an odd collection of mismatched furniture—a big comfortable-looking recliner, a cozy love seat and a carved French walnut settee covered in ivory dam-ask of the type favored by June, and presumably Charmaine.

Above the mantel hung a studio portrait of Charmaine. Her perfect features and lustrous long blond hair sparked a familiar upwelling of envy and admiration. Ridiculous, Nicola thought, to feel jealous of a dead woman but there it was. At the same time, she wished Charmaine were here, filling the house with her infectious laughter and outrageous schemes for fun.

Emily crouched before the fireplace, hands up to the feeble warmth given off by the barely glowing embers. "It's cold."

Nicola pulled the heavy drapes shut against the gathering dusk, tucking in the voluminous lace curtains that had grown dusty through neglect. Then she took a handful of kindling from the basket by the fireplace and levered open the stove's door to throw them in. A few healthy blows with the bellows and the kindling crackled into flames. She stacked a couple of larger logs at angles and shut the door.

Emily inched closer and sat on her heels, holding her hands in front of the heated glass.

Nicola got out her Nikon single lens reflex and perched on the settee. The couch was hard, as if it had been stuffed with horse hair, and so high Nicola's feet barely touched the floor. Moving to the love seat, she sank into the soft cushions and began to rewind the film she'd shot that day.

"Were those your mother's?" she asked Emily even though she could tell at a glance the crystal figurines ranged along the mantelpiece were pure Charmaine. There was a prancing unicorn, a ballerina balanced delicately on one pointed toe, a pair of leaping dolphins in a spray of blue crystal water and many other dainty and fragile designs.

"Yes," Emily said, nodding solemnly. "Daddy says we have to take care of them and make sure none get broken."

Nicola removed the spent roll and clicked a new film into place. Then she raised the camera and snapped a photo of Emily, capturing the warm flicker of orange and yellow illuminating her round face. Emily looked up in surprise at the flash and smiled. Nicola refocused and clicked again.

Setting the camera on the coffee table, Nicola said, "What do you usually do after school?"

"It's my job to feed the fish." Emily got the container of fish food from the cabinet beneath the tank. She sprinkled a pinch on the surface of the water then watched the fish swim up and snatch at the flakes.

"What kind are they?" Nicola asked, bending over, hands on knees to watch, too.

"There's two angelfishes, five neon tetras and a sucker fish. We used to have a Siamese fighting fish, but he kept biting the angelfishes' tails so Daddy took him back to the store."

Nicola straightened and wandered over to the shelving unit. Her fingers grazed the ivory glaze on a large ceramic pot with a lid. "This is pretty."

Emily gazed up at her solemnly. "Mommy's in there."

Nicola snatched her hand away and pressed it to her heart. "Oh, you mean her ashes."

Slightly shaken she moved across to where Aidan's trophies were displayed. Judging by the inscriptions on the gilt cups he'd had some impressive wins in major national and international competitions. "Does your dad still race?"

Emily said something in her soft voice Nicola didn't catch. "Pardon?" Nicola asked.

"No, he doesn't race," the girl said a little louder.

Nicola sat on the wide arm of the chair. "Sometimes little girls have to roar to make themselves heard."

Emily smiled uncertainly. "Like a lion?"

"Exactly. Let me hear you roar."

"Roar," Emily said in just a slightly more powerful than normal voice.

"No, I mean, roar," she said, making a hearty growl. "Like that."

Emily giggled. "Roar!"

"That's better." Nicola smiled.

Emily pretended to pounce on her. "Roar! Roar! Roar!"

Nicola laughed. "Okay, that's enough for now. Shall we go make that snowman?"

"First I need a snack. Toasted cheese. Come, I'll show you." Emily took her by the hand and led her to the kitchen.

Nicola was an indifferent cook, but she followed orders well. Her toasted cheese made under the broiler and hot chocolate with three marshmallows were happily in accordance with Miss Emily's exacting taste.

"I don't have school tomorrow," Emily announced. "It's a curr-curr—"

"Curriculum day?" Nicola guessed.

Emily nodded. "There's a notice in my backpack."

"We could go up the mountain," Nicola suggested. "Would you like that?"

Emily's eyes lit and she smiled, her chocolate moustache widening. "Yes, please!" Her smile faded. "I don't know if Daddy will let me."

"You be sure and ask him tonight. Do you have skis?" Emily shook her head. "Never mind, we can rent."

When they were warmed inside and out, they put their outdoor clothes back on. Nicola slung her camera over her neck and they went into the front yard. Snow was falling in big fluffy flakes.

AIDAN PULLED INTO his driveway to find a half-finished snowman crouched fatly on the buried lawn, its head at its feet. Aidan's glance went automatically toward his study window but no small nose was pressed against the pane. A small surge of panic, quickly repressed, tightened his chest.

Then a snowball hit the Land Cruiser with a resounding *thwack*. Aidan started and peered into the dark corners of the yard. *Thwack.* Another snowball and another. Then girlish squeals of laughter.

Aidan got out of the truck and Emily appeared and openly threw snowballs. "Roar!"

Nicola was hiding behind the snowman, making more to hand to her.

Aidan advanced in a hail of snowballs and scooped up an armful of snow. Laughing, he charged his daughter and dumped his load on top of her head. "That'll teach you to mess with your daddy."

A snowball struck the back of his neck, sending an icy trickle down his collar. Slowly he turned. Nicola had her hand over her mouth, her eyes dancing in the porch light. In her down jacket and snowpants her body looked bulky and shapeless. Slowly he started walking toward her, not sure what he was going to do, but aware he wasn't going to let her get away with that!

Hands raised now, she backed away. "Just kidding! We can stop now. I'm done."

"I'm not." He gathered up more snow and advanced on Nicola. Behind him Emily giggled and pelted him with tiny snowballs that splatted against his back. Nicola continued to retreat until she came up against the prickly branches of a blue spruce.

He lunged, grabbing her around the waist in an iron grip and washed her face with snow.

"Hey!" Spluttering and laughing, Nicola struggled and kicked. One booted foot connected with his shin and he leaped back, yelping in pain as he clutched his leg and hopped about. Emily threw herself at him, knocking him off balance. He fell into a snowdrift. Nicola seized the advantage and piled more snow on him.

"Two against one. No fair," he protested, attempting to fend off Emily. He lifted her in the air, arms and legs waving, and got to his feet.

Aidan set his daughter down and glanced from her to Nicola. "Truce?"

Emily jumped up and down. "We won! We won!" She tugged on his jacket. "Help us finish the snowman, Daddy."

"Did this poor fellow lose his head over a

woman?" Aidan asked, picking up the basketball-size lump of snow.

"It *is* a woman," Emily shrieked. "Can't you tell?"

He stood back. Sure enough, on second glance, the snow figure had a distinctly matronly shape. Teasing, he said, "No wonder she hasn't got a brain."

"Them's fightin' words," Nicola warned, reaching for more snow.

Grinning, Aidan sidled toward her again, hefting the snow woman's head in one hand.

"You wouldn't dare." Nicola's eyes widened in alarm.

"Wouldn't I?"

"Daddy!" Emily planted her hands on her hips and glared at him. "Put the snow woman's head on her body!"

"Okay, you little tyrant," he said good-naturedly. He balanced the head on top of the body and packed extra snow into the groove to keep it attached. "How was school today?"

"We made Christmas cards and colored in a big picture of Santa and his reindeer…." Her words trailed off as she busily rolled snow into a ball across the lawn. "Now I'm making a snow baby."

Nicola bent to pick up a scarf lying on the ground and tied it around the snow woman's neck. Aidan found a few pieces of gravel at the edge of the drive-way and pressed them into the head, creating a face.

"How did everything go today?" he asked.

Nicola glanced up. "Fine. I had a chat with Emily's teacher. Sara Winston taught me fifth grade way back when."

"Oh?" he said warily. Sara was great with the kids, but he'd noticed in his parent-teacher meeting she had a tendency to be indiscreet, often blurting out information about other families she had no right to pass on. "What did she have to say?"

Nicola lowered her voice and looked him directly in the eye. "She said there was some controversy sur-rounding Charmaine's death."

Great. Nicola'd been here barely twenty-four hours and already the rumor mill had found fresh ears. "There was a lot of unsubstantiated gossip. What exactly did she tell you?"

"That some people think you pushed Charmaine off the mountain." Nicola, her wet hair plastered to a thin oval face with a pointed chin, looked like a mere girl but her clear-eyed gaze was anything but ingenuous. "Did you?"

Her directness caught him off guard. But in some ways it was easier to deal with than oblique looks and innuendo. Returning her gaze steadily, he replied, "No."

"Of course, you'd claim that even if you had," she said matter-of-factly.

He shrugged, pretending it didn't matter one way or another. "True."

"Don't you care what people say about you?"

He'd rather they talked about him than discover the truth about Charmaine. "I learned long ago that people will think what they want to think." He paused as Emily came back their way pushing a lumpy sphere of snow. "This discussion isn't appropriate in front of my daughter."

"Of course." Nicola scooped up more snow to pack onto the snow woman's torso, sculpting it into an arm.

"Will you be looking after Emily again tomorrow?" he asked.

Nicola nodded. "Apparently the Christmas Ball is bigger than King Kong. June's taken charge of half a dozen subcommittees."

"I'm not surprised." He couldn't hide a trace of rancor. "With her need for control she should have been CEO of some big company."

Nicola was silent a moment. "You don't like her."

"She doesn't like me."

"Why?"

This was the oddest conversation he'd had in a long time. He shrugged. "It has to do with Charmaine."

"In what way?"

Couldn't she tell it was personal? Did she really think he was going to unburden himself about Charmaine after knowing her for twenty-four hours when he'd spent the past six years bottling things up inside, not confiding even in his family?

He created a smoke screen by elaborating on a pet peeve. "June means well but she spoils Emily. She's already given her enough presents for two Christmases and the holiday is still weeks away. I was glad you took over, even temporarily."

Nicola smiled. "I'm loving it. Emily's a doll."

"She seems to have taken to you." He paused. "I understand you and Charmaine were very close. Forgive me, but it seems odd when you and she are so… different."

"Like night and day," Nicola said dryly. "Charmaine got all the boys—when she was around no one noticed me."

"Come on, I'll bet a cute girl like you must have had swarms of guys hanging around," Aidan said gallantly.

"If I was so cute why weren't *you* hanging around?"

Flummoxed, Aidan stared. "Me? I didn't know you—"

"Existed?" She smiled wryly and turned to Emily

who was trying to heave a large ball. "My point, exactly. Don't worry, I got used to living in Charmaine's shadow. It doesn't bother me anymore." She turned to Emily who was trying to heave a large ball of snow onto the base she'd made. "You're making that snow baby all by yourself. Can I help?"

"Yes." Emily stopped and panted. "Put that on top. And it's not a snow baby anymore, it's a snow lion."

"I've heard of snow leopards," Aidan said.

"No, it's a lion," Emily declared. "Honestly, Daddy."

Nicola's amused gaze met Aidan's over his daughter's head.

"You're not in high school anymore," he said. "Are you married?" She shook her head. "Boyfriend? If I'm being too nosy just tell me to mind my own business."

"That's okay," she said easily. "I don't have time for a boyfriend. This photography assignment will keep me busy for quite some time."

"Where do you go after here?"

"Banff, Tahoe, Vail, Aspen—I can't remember the entire itinerary. We're covering all the major resorts in a coffee-table book for ski buffs."

"Pity it won't be ready in time for Christmas."

She smiled. "It will be. Next year."

"What am I going to use for whiskers?" Emily demanded.

Aidan turned only to find she was asking Nicola. One day, he marveled, and this quiet woman had completely won over his daughter. He watched Nicola help Emily gather needles from a clear patch of ground near the base of a pine tree and press them into the cat's face.

Leaving the child, Nicola got up and came back to where he was standing. "I'd better get going," she said. "You look half frozen and your dinner is waiting."

"Why don't you stay and eat with us?"

"Thanks, but June and Roy are going to be home late and I told my aunt I'd make dinner." She turned to Emily. "Bye, possum. See you tomorrow."

Aidan walked Nicola to her car, thinking back to the first part of their conversation and feeling the need to convince her of his innocence. He opened the door for her, but before she could climb in, he touched her shoulder, stopping her. "I loved Charmaine with all my heart."

Her brows came together in a puzzled frown, her searching gaze quietly alert. "Everyone loved Charmaine."

Aidan watched her get into her vehicle and start the engine. Although she hadn't said so, he got the distinct impression Nicola was reserving judgment about him. He got that a lot from people he didn't know and over the years he'd learned not to care. For some reason, it bothered him coming from Nicola.

CHAPTER FOUR

NICOLA ARRIVED HOME to a dark and empty house. Pushing aside thoughts of Aidan's warm fire and delicious-smelling stew she peeled off her wet outer clothing and went to the kitchen to start dinner.

June seemed to have every gadget known to man lining her granite countertops, but from the pristine condition of the appliances, Nicola deduced she rarely used them. Luckily the ingredients for one of Nicola's small repertoire of foolproof dishes—spaghetti bolognese—were on hand. Nicola got out onions, garlic and mushrooms, had a look at the food processor, and decided a knife and chopping board were easier to clean.

Aidan had been forthright about the rumors surrounding Charmaine's death, she mused as she peeled the papery skin off the onion. Yet she had the feeling he was hiding something regarding Charmaine.

Six years was a long time. Aidan was a good-looking man. Why hadn't he married again? Nicola didn't think it could be due to a lack of interested and available women. Was he still grieving? Or did he find it hard to move on because he was guilty?

Tears from the onion vapors slid down her cheeks and she wiped her eyes with the cuff of her long-sleeved thermal shirt. She quickly chopped the mushrooms and green pepper and added them to the pot along with the hamburger meat and a couple tins of tomatoes. The big stockpot of water she'd set on the stove was boiling so she dumped in a package of dried spaghetti and gave it a stir.

That done she ran upstairs to get a book to read while she waited for June and Roy. Her footsteps slowed as she passed Charmaine's closed door. The cuckoo clock on the wall behind her ticked loudly in the silence. Why wasn't Emily allowed in her mother's old room?

Nicola reached out and turned the handle. The room was dark and with no light on in the hall she could only make out the vague shapes of a bed and dresser, desk and chair. She felt for the light switch and flicked it on.

Nicola gasped.

Charmaine's room looked exactly as it had in high school, from the frilly pink curtains and matching bedspread right down to old pop-star posters and her cheerleader pom-poms. Incredulous, Nicola went farther into the room, drawn to the dressing table where her cousin had spent hours practicing applying makeup and the latest hairstyles. Unlike in high school when the dressing table's surface was a jumble of mascara tubes, lipsticks and hairbrushes everything was meticulously arranged like a…a shrine.

A large, framed photo of Charmaine's graduation portrait, forever young, eternally beautiful, held center stage. She was heartbreakingly lovely, Nicola thought. Would it be any wonder if Aidan had fallen so deeply in love he couldn't get over her, even six years later?

To the right of the photo was a lock of golden curling hair tied up in a pink ribbon, to the left a cluster of dried rosebuds—from her prom corsage? In front, a baby bracelet with the letters of her name picked out in black on tiny white beads. Bronze baby shoes, a heart-shaped locket, a smaller photograph of Charmaine with her mother and father, a cone of incense in a small brass slipper.

Nicola held the incense to her nose. Jasmine. She smiled, remembering Charmaine's youthful passion for everything jasmine—incense, tea, perfume… she'd even wanted to change her name to Jasmine when she grew up.

Replacing the incense Nicola picked up the locket. Inside were tiny photos of Charmaine and her.

Tears of sorrow and loss washed away the last bitter traces of the onion. In spite of their different personalities she and Charmaine had indeed been inseparable, confiding in each other all their girlish dreams and desires. Somehow she'd never found another friend that had been able to match the closeness she'd had with Charmaine. She snapped the locket shut with a small click and set it carefully back on the dressing table.

Nicola sat on the bed and picked up a teddy bear from the lace-edged pillow. She couldn't imagine Uncle Roy, austere and remote in his insurance man's suit, arranging teenage memorabilia or—Nicola wiped a finger across the polished maple bedside table—dusting regularly. No, June must have done this. She and Charmaine had always been close, the more so because Charmaine was the only child and took after June in looks and temperament.

The front door opened. Nicola heard footsteps moving between the hall and the kitchen and got up to go greet her aunt and uncle. As she came out of Charmaine's room she heard a commotion of clattering pots and excited voices. Oh, no! The pasta.

Nicola raced downstairs and stopped dead in the kitchen doorway. The spaghetti was boiling over, froth and scalding water pouring down the sides of the pot and onto the floor. June was at the stove, sliding the pot off the heat.

"Oh my gosh! I'm so sorry!" Nicola exclaimed. "Where's the mop?"

"It's in the cupboard in the laundry room," June called.

Nicola grabbed the mop and raced back to the kitchen. June turned around to face Nicola and her face went white.

"It's all my fault," Nicola apologized again. "I wanted to have dinner ready when you and Uncle Roy came—"

June shook her head, speechless, and pointed her finger at Nicola. Nicola looked down. She still had Charmaine's stuffed bear clasped in one arm.

"Oh, that," she said, relieved no further harm had been done. "It's just a teddy bear."

June swallowed with apparent difficulty. "No one. *No one,*" she emphasized, "is allowed in my baby's room."

Oh, dear. "I didn't move anything except for the bear," Nicola told June apologetically. "I'll put it back right now."

"I'll do it." June crossed the kitchen and took the bear from Nicola's unprotesting grasp.

Her uncle Roy, solid in blue pinstripe, came into the room. "When will dinner be ready?" Silence followed his query. He looked over his glasses at his wife holding the bear. "Never mind."

Nodding vaguely, he went to the glass-fronted cabinet beside the fridge and took out a crystal tumbler. "Er, Scotch, anyone?"

June brushed past him into the hall without reply.

"No, thanks." Nicola ran upstairs after her aunt then paused in the doorway to Charmaine's room.

June was bent over the bed, carefully positioning the bear in his place atop the satin-cased pillow. Tenderly she adjusted the pink bow around his neck so the loops were perfectly flat and not twisted.

"Aunt June…"

June straightened and turned, her face calm. "It's all right, Nicola. No harm done. I should have mentioned that this room was off-limits. I thought the shut door was indication enough." She glanced around as if checking that everything else was in place. Apparently satisfied, her shoulders relaxed.

Nicola stepped inside the room and shut the door. "Can we talk?"

June stiffened again. "Dinner—"

"It can wait a few minutes." Nicola took her hands. "Please."

"Your uncle is allowed one drink before dinner," June informed her, maintaining her erect posture.

"If the meal is delayed, he'll have two. It's not good for his heart. The doctor said—"

Nicola dropped her aunt's hands and pulled her into a hug. "You poor thing. Losing Charmaine must have been so awful for you."

June sagged in her arms and drew in a long ragged sigh. "Oh, Nic, I miss her so much. She was my beautiful little girl. Why did she have to die?"

"It was an accident," Nicola said, holding her. Even as she spoke, she wondered if that were true.

June drew back, shaking her head. "Aidan was right beside her when she went off the cliff. Why couldn't he have saved her?"

"I don't know," Nicola said miserably. "Didn't anyone ask him?"

"He said it all happened too quickly."

"Maybe it did. If she slipped and lost her balance…" She trailed off, shuddering at the image those thoughts conjured. Charmaine falling off the cliff onto rocks. A powder-blue ski suit, stained red. Golden hair matted with blood.

"Why was she off the groomed ski trail?" June went on doggedly. Nicola got the impression she'd asked these same questions a million times. "Why was she even in the permanently closed area?"

"Was she?" Nicola said sharply. "I didn't know that."

Her aunt nodded. "Aidan knew better than to take anyone there, even an expert skier like Charmaine."

"Why did he?"

"He says he didn't. He says he found her there and was trying to get her to come out." June plucked a tissue from the box on the dresser and blew her nose. "Charmaine wouldn't have gone out of bounds. She never did anything against the rules."

Nicola thought of the times her cousin had coaxed her into skipping school to hitchhike into Squamish and hang out at the Dairy Queen. "We don't always know people as well as we think we do."

"I know my little girl," June said firmly. "She was a loving wife and devoted mother. I know that if Aidan had taken proper care of her she would be alive today."

There was a long silence during which Nicola worked up the courage to ask in a cracked whisper, "Do *you* believe he pushed her?"

"Yes. No. Maybe. Oh, I don't know what to believe. He should have taken better care of Charmaine," June complained. "He left her alone too much."

"Could she have committed…" Nicola could hardly bear to say the word suicide. She didn't need to. One look at her aunt's horrified expression told her June knew what she was trying to say—and disagreed vehemently.

"Absolutely not," June said. "Charmaine had it all—a devoted husband she adored, a brand-new baby she loved to distraction. Even with Emily's health problems—"

"Emily had problems?" Nicola asked. "Dad never told me that."

"It was nothing serious," June said dismissively. "I didn't tell Stan—what could he do down there in Australia?"

"He's family, and would want to know," Nicola demurred quietly. "What was wrong with Emily?"

"Oh, I hardly remember," June said. "Something to do with her spine, a developmental thing. She's fine now."

"Still, Charmaine would have been upset," Nicola said. "She was so squeamish about sickness or injury."

"Charmaine was strong," June contradicted. "She was devoted to that baby."

"I'm sure she was," Nicola said soothingly. She thought of the letters her cousin had written during her pregnancy, full of happiness and anticipation. Nicola had thought it odd the letters had stopped once Charmaine had given birth but had attributed it to the heavy demands of a new baby. Now the lapse made even more sense; Charmaine was busy caring for a sick child with no time to write.

"Well," June said, blotting her eyes with another

tissue. "Let's have dinner before Roy gets sloshed. I don't want to lose him, too."

Nicola went out and waited for her aunt to turn off the light and close the door behind her. "He's a grown man. Can't he self-regulate?"

June rolled her eyes. "My dear, he's a baby. If it wasn't for me he wouldn't get dressed in the morning."

Nicola said nothing, thinking it was sad that June overestimated her late daughter and underestimated everyone else.

AIDAN DISHED UP BEEF STEW on bone-china plates; Charmaine had refused to eat off anything less and Aidan had never gotten around to buying stoneware. The plates, like the crystal figurines, weren't to his taste, but he kept them. The self-help books his mother had given him after Charmaine's death suggested he not make major changes in his life for at least a year. One year had turned into six and Aidan had fallen into a deadly inertia, oblivious to his surroundings.

"Stew again," Emily complained with a quiet sigh. "Nicola said she was going to make spaghetti for their dinner."

"We had spaghetti last week," he reminded her.

"Yes, but not like Nicola's."

"What is Nicola's spaghetti like?" he asked patiently.

"I don't know. It's just different."

"Eat up, sweetheart, or we'll end up having stew tomorrow, too."

Emily sighed and went back to her meal. Aidan's thoughts went back to revolving around his dilemma. Should he apply for the assistant manager's position or should he let it go? He wanted the job, rather badly, he realized, for the recognition of his expertise and experience. Also it would give him a chance to implement his ideas for improving conditions for the patrollers and safety for skiers. Last but not least, he could use the extra money the promotion would bring.

He leaned over and twitched back the lace curtains, another legacy of Charmaine, to reveal the snow-covered expanse of Alta Lake visible under a rising moon. The neighborhood children had cleared a makeshift skating rink complete with two battered, netless goals. Sometimes he wished he was a kid again, with nothing more on his mind than looking forward to playing hockey after school.

"Can I, Daddy? Nicola told me I should ask you," Emily said in her soft voice.

"Sure, honey," Aidan replied automatically then realized guiltily he'd been so lost in thought he didn't know what she'd said.

Before he could find out what he'd just agreed to

there was a knock at the door. A second later it opened and his brother Nate called out. "Anybody home?"

"In the dining room," Aidan said. "Grab a plate from the kitchen."

Nate, his dark hair tousled from pushing the hood of his heavy parka off his forehead, appeared in the doorway. "Can't stay. Angela and I just got back from Vancouver and I wanted to drop off the book on tropical fish you ordered." He tugged on one of Emily's blond braids. "How's my girl?"

Emily dimpled up at him. "Fine, thank you, Unca Nate."

"How's the new store doing?" Aidan asked. Nate's Whistler Village mountain-bike shop had proven such a success that he'd recently expanded his business with a second store in Vancouver. Due to Angela's job as marketing director at a business-woman's magazine, they spent a few days a month in the city, staying at an apartment Angela had before she and Nate got back together.

"Turnover is brisk thanks to a great location and Rachel's proving to be an excellent manager." Nate started to leave then paused. "Almost forgot. Angela wanted me to ask you and Emily for dinner tomorrow."

"I don't know about a late night for Emily," Aidan began.

"It's Friday and Emily can always go to sleep in our bed if she gets tired. I've got to warn you, though, Angela's trying out a new recipe."

"Uh-oh." Aidan knew all about Angela's disastrous cooking attempts and considered his health-food-conscious brother not only brave but lucky to have survived so far unscathed. The problem in Aidan's opinion was that Angela was too ambitious, cooking complicated dishes while lacking basic skills.

"She's getting better, honest," Nate said, grinning. Outside, a horn tooted. "She ran into Nicola at the school and invited her, too. So will you come?"

The prospect of meeting Nicola there tipped the scales. If she got to know him in the context of his family and friends she'd see he wasn't the bad person June had no doubt painted him. Maybe he shouldn't care what Nicola thought, but he did.

"All right," Aidan said. "Thanks."

IN BED THAT NIGHT Nicola reread Charmaine's letters from start to finish, looking for any evidence, no matter how slight, that despite June's assurances to the contrary, her cousin might have been tempted to take her own life. The notion was far-fetched but not completely implausible. If Aidan had witnessed his wife's suicide that might be what he was covering up.

But Nicola could find nothing to suggest Charmaine had contemplated such a thing for even one second. Nicola sighed and put the letters away.

She turned out the light and fell asleep quickly, only to wake again at 4:30 a.m. She went downstairs in her pajamas for a glass of water. Roy, portly and graying, was seated at the kitchen table in his dressing gown and slippers, drinking Mylanta from the bottle.

"Are you having trouble sleeping, too?" he asked sympathetically.

"Jet lag." Nicola took a glass from the cupboard and filled it at the tap. She leaned against the counter and drank, watching her uncle over the rim of her tumbler. He looked tired and old, the lines of his face etched deep, so different from the jovial character she remembered as a child.

"At home in Australia we had no idea there was controversy surrounding Charmaine's death," she said. "What do *you* think happened to her, Uncle Roy?"

He took another swig of the liquid antacid and grimaced as it went down. "I don't know. All I know is June hasn't been the same since Charmaine passed away." He looked at the Mylanta bottle and sighed. "Neither have I."

Nicola asked a few more questions but her uncle

seemed disinclined to answer. "If you want the facts," he said, "why don't you check out the newspaper archives at the public library?"

After he shuffled back up to his room Nicola wrapped herself in a wool throw to sit in front of the cold fire to wait for Emily. As the quiet minutes ticked by she decided that the first chance she got she would do as Roy suggested. She owed it to her cousin to find out exactly what had happened up on Whistler Mountain. Why *had* Charmaine died with an experienced ski patroller at her side and everything to live for?

CHAPTER FIVE

NICOLA WAS DRAWN downstairs later that morning by the aroma of freshly brewed coffee. She found June seated at the table in a tailored red suit, going over a checklist of tasks related to the Christmas Ball and murmuring to herself, "Decorations, food, drink…"

"Good morning," Nicola said, pouring herself a cup of coffee. "I forgot to mention yesterday that Angela Wilde invited me to dinner tonight. Is that okay?"

Negligently June lifted one shoulder. "You're perfectly free to have dinner with whomever you like. Just so you know, those Wildes stick together."

Nicola spooned sugar into her cup. "Meaning…?"

"Nothing." June gathered up her papers and placed them neatly in a leather folder. From a slot in the inside cover she removed a thin cardboard rectangle and handed it to Nicola. "I got you a ticket to the Christmas Ball."

"Thanks, Aunt June, but I didn't bring any fancy

dresses with me on this trip." Nicola didn't bother to mention she didn't *own* any evening gowns. Ankle-length cotton dresses suitable for keeping cool on a hot summer day—yes. Fancy silk and satin—no way.

"Don't worry," June said. "You can borrow something of Charmaine's."

Nicola choked on her first sip of hot coffee. *"Charmaine's?"* she repeated incredulously. "You still have some of her clothes?"

"I have *all* her clothes." June crossed to put her cup into the dishwasher. "I made Aidan bring them to me after the funeral. I was afraid he'd give them to one of the charities and I'd be tortured by the sight of strange women walking around town squeezed into my darling's outfits." She glanced at her watch and added, "Is Emily up? It's almost time to leave for school."

"She's getting dressed, but not for school. It's a curriculum day." Nicola set out a bowl and cereal on the table then went back up stairs.

While Emily ate breakfast, Nicola sifted through the contents of her suitcase, hoping that while she wasn't looking some unknown fairy godmother had packed a long gown. Almost anything would be preferable to wearing one of her cousin's old dresses. Not that it wouldn't be perfectly gorgeous but it wouldn't fit. Plus, there was something creepy about the idea of wearing Charmaine's clothing even though Nicola had spent the better part of her teenage years wishing she *was* Charmaine.

She dug through blue jeans and tracksuits, sweat-shirts and flannel shirts, wool pants and sweaters. She even had a drab but serviceable pantsuit for meeting with the editor when they got to New York. But no finery suitable for anything so grand as a ball.

With a sigh she sat back on her heels and regarded the mess dismally. Face it, she was no fashionista and she'd long ago given up any aspirations along those lines. She would simply tell June that balls and ball gowns weren't her cup of tea. That was true enough.

An hour later Nicola and Emily jumped off the Fitzimmons Express chairlift at Olympic Station on the lower slopes of Whistler Mountain. The mountain was blindingly white under a bright winter sun and, with a thick dusting of new snow on a thirty-inch base, ski conditions were perfect.

Nicola rented skis for them both. She was surprised when she had to show Emily how to clamp her ski boot into the binding. "Does your dad usually do this for you?" she asked.

Emily shook her head. "I've never been skiing."

"What—never?" Nicola could hardly believe it. She'd assumed Aidan would have taught his daughter to ski from an early age. Clearly, she'd been wrong.

"Daddy never takes me on the mountain in winter," Emily went on. "He says it's too dangerous. He doesn't even let me go for a ride on the chairlift."

Oh, great. Nicola scratched her head under her polar fleece cap. What should she do—turn around now and go back down the mountain? "Did he say you could go today?"

Emily nodded. "Maybe because *you're* taking me he said 'yes' this time."

"Maybe," Nicola said doubtfully. They were all suited up, ready to ski. It would be a shame to go home. "Or maybe he thinks you're big enough now. Let's get that boot clamped in. Push hard."

Emily made another unsuccessful attempt before quitting in frustration. "I can't do it."

"Try again," Nicola insisted gently.

"You do it for me."

"Give it one more go."

Her bottom lip jutting mutinously Emily angrily pushed down on the clamp. "It won't go—" Even as she spoke, the binding clicked into place. "I did it!" She grinned up at Nicola triumphantly.

"I knew you could."

Nicola led the way across to a short gentle slope where the smallest children learned to ski. Scores of kids were sliding erratically to the bottom. The odd young hotshot zipped down the hill, zigzagging in and out of the less advanced skiers.

A man in mirrored sunglasses and a red and gray jacket with a white cross on the back whooshed past with casual speed.

"Daddy," Emily cried out.

The patroller ignored her and kept on going.

"That wasn't your dad," said Nicola, who'd got a good look at the face and the fringe of light brown hair beneath the dark hat.

Standing at the top of the bunny hill, Emily looked very small in her red snowsuit and multicolored knitted cap. "It's a long way down," she said. "And steep."

To Nicola the slope looked almost flat. "Don't worry. I'll be with you the whole time. You'll be quite safe."

She showed the girl how to bend her knees and turn. "Push off with your poles then keep your arms tucked in close. When you want to stop, push the tips of your skis together like a snowplow. Are you ready?"

Emily nodded, mute with excitement.

"Away we go!" Nicola pushed off and started down the hill. They'd only gone a few yards before Emily hit the first baby-size mogul and fell. She slid on her snowsuit a dozen feet before Nicola could stop her.

"Are you all right?" Nicola helped her up.

Her hat askew, the girl nodded, eager to try again. On her next attempt, Emily found her voice, emitting semicontinuous screams of delight as she slipped and slid down hill. They'd almost made it to the bottom without another fall when a boy of about ten hurtled down the hill on an oblique trajectory that Nicola could see would result in collision with Emily.

"Look out," she yelled, to no avail. The boy clearly wasn't in control. Nicola tried to get between Emily and the boy, but another child skied into her path. The boy was now close enough for her to see the alarm in his white-rimmed eyes. There was only one thing to do. Lunging forward she grabbed Emily by the back of her snowsuit and skidded to a stop. Off balance, Nicola fell. Emily was thrown face-down a few feet away in a tangled, snow-covered heap. Her boot came away from the bindings and one tiny ski slid to the bottom on its own.

"Emily!" Nicola's heart beat in sudden fright as she crawled forward and turned the girl over. "Speak to me!"

Emily's apple-cheeked face split in an enormous laughing grin. "That was so fun! Let's do it again!"

Nicola hugged her. "You bet." She glanced up the hill at the pint-size skiers heading their way. "We've got to get over to the side. When I say go… Run!"

Emily pushed with her foot and half slid, half ran, to the other side of the slope. Nicola was laughing helplessly and telling her to wait there while she retrieved her other ski when a patroller skidded to a stop in front of them in a spray of snow.

"Thanks!" Nicola exclaimed, noticing he was holding the wayward ski. "I was just going after that...."

Her words trailed off. This time it *was* Aidan.

"Hi," Nicola said, caught in midgiggle. Her idiotic grin was reflected in his mirrored sunglasses. "Care to take a turn on the bunny hill with us?"

"What do you think you're doing?" His cheeks were flushed and his breath emerged in puffs of condensation from the angry slash of his mouth.

Her smile faded. "What do you mean?"

"This!" He jabbed a ski pole at his daughter. "I saw you crash on the hill and just about had a heart attack. Emily is a small child. She's delicate. She most definitely isn't allowed to take part in dangerous activities. I can't believe you brought her up the mountain without asking my permission."

"I can't believe a child of yours doesn't know how to ski," Nicola countered, bewildered by his attitude. "We did ask your permission, at least Emily did. She said you told her it was okay."

"I said nothing of the sort."

Nicola turned to the girl who was still struggling to clamp her boot back onto the ski binding. Feeling the adults' gazes on her, she glanced up fearfully.

"It's okay, honey." Nicola crouched to look the little girl in the face. "Tell me again, what did you say and what did your dad say when you asked him about skiing?"

Emily glanced from Nicola to her glowering father and said nothing. Nicola shook her head in disgust at Aidan's overblown reaction. "You're scaring her."

Aidan crouched in front of Emily, too. "I'm not angry with *you,* sweetheart. When did you ask me about skiing?"

"Last night at dinner." Emily was near tears. "I said Nicola wanted to take me and I asked, 'Can I go, Daddy?' And you said, 'yes.'"

Nicola saw his expression change as recollection of the exchange fell into place. Then he covered his face with his hand as if to scrub away the evidence of his mistake. "I wasn't really listening to what you were saying. I didn't know what I was agreeing to."

"But you *said...*" Emily protested.

"I know. It's not your fault." Aidan rose slowly to his feet and turned to Nicola. "I guess it's not your fault, either. Still, she's too young. I don't want her on this mountain."

"Sure, we took a spill but there was no harm done," Nicola began incredulously.

"*This* time. You were lucky. If that boy had run over her hand, or knocked her head with his ski…" A shudder ran across his shoulders. "I could hear her screaming all over the mountain."

"Wasn't that great?" Nicola challenged him. "It's about time she learned to utter a sound above a whisper."

"You scared the daylights out of her."

"She loved it. Didn't you, Emily?" Emily nodded. Nicola turned back to Aidan. "*You're* the one who's scared."

"I'm her father. It's my duty and responsibility to ensure her safety. I'm on this mountain every day. I see accidents you wouldn't believe. Heads split open, broken femurs jutting through skin—"

"Stop! Now *you're* scaring her," Nicola said. "I'm sure accidents do happen but you can't wrap her in cotton wool and protect her from every bump and scratch."

"Why not?" he demanded.

Nicola stared at him and spread her hands helplessly. "Because it's not healthy. You should be teaching her, not hiding her away."

"Don't turn this into a critique of my parenting skills. *You* shouldn't have relied on the word of a six-year-old when it came to making the decision to go skiing. You should have asked me yourself for permission."

"Maybe I should have," Nicola conceded. "But I still say you're overprotective. No wonder Emily's shy and timid."

"My daughter's personality is no concern of yours." His hands clenched around his ski poles. "Thank you for looking after Emily but your help isn't needed anymore."

Aidan held out his hand to his daughter. "Come, Em. You can stay in the dispatcher's office until I'm done for the day. You remember Christy. She's looked after you before in an emergency."

Emily obediently took his hand, accepting that her father's word was law and that he knew best, but she glanced back at Nicola with big sad eyes.

Shocked by the sudden turn of events, Nicola skied after them. "This is crazy. You don't have to take her away. We'll stop skiing. We'll go home and bake cookies."

"Please, Daddy?" Emily begged.

"Not today." He hoisted his daughter effortlessly into his arms. "I want you where I know you're safe."

Emily leaned forlornly over her father's shoulder and waved goodbye to Nicola as Aidan tucked his poles under his other arm and skied off.

Nicola stood alone in the snow and waved back. Flakes of snow began to fall in light drifts, covering her shoulders in a thin blanket. In a last attempt to make him see reason, she called, "You're overreacting!"

Her words were lost amid the happy shouts and laughter of children on the slope.

"ARE YOU READY?" Aidan poked his head into his daughter's room. "We're going to Nate and Angela's for dinner."

"I'm ready." Emily was seated on the floor having a tea party with three of her favorite dolls. Her hair was tangled and wet from her bath and she wore a towel wrapped around her.

Aidan shook his head with an indulgent smile and went to her white-painted dresser to find her clothes. "What would you like to wear, the blue outfit or the purple?"

"Blue." She bent closer to the doll on her right to whisper something then bent her ear to listen to the reply.

He laid out underpants, socks, blue stretch pants and a blue long-sleeve top on the pink gingham bedspread and left her with a reminder they'd be leaving in ten minutes.

When he came back she had her underwear and

one sock on and was offering her blond doll a Ritz cracker on a tiny plastic plate. Aidan sat on the bed and held out her pants. "Come here and put these on."

She struggled into her pants, hopping up and down to tug them up around her waist. "Why can't I go skiing, Daddy? Nicola was sad when I left."

Aidan handed her the shirt then helped pull it down over her head. He suspected Nicola was more angry than sad but he wasn't responsible for Nicola's feelings, whatever they were. "I was worried about you."

"We were having fun." Her head popped through, hair tousled.

He smoothed her fine blond hair away from her eyes. "Just before your mom died I told her I'd never let anything happen to you. Ever."

"She loved me lots," Emily stated confidently.

Aidan pulled his daughter into a hug so she wouldn't see the pain in his eyes. "More than anything else in the world."

Warm yellow light glowed in the front windows of Nate and Angela's two-story log home on Alta Lake Road when Aidan pulled into the gravel driveway fifteen minutes later. Parked there already was June's Suburban.

Aidan groaned inwardly. The last person he wanted to see right now was Nicola. No doubt the feeling was mutual. He'd been half-hoping Nicola would cancel. He might have done so himself except Nate would have demanded an explanation and Aidan had the feeling his reasons for dismissing Nicola wouldn't sound nearly as reasonable as they had this morning on the ski hill. So much for showing her his other side. He didn't know what he was thinking on that score, anyway. What did he care what she thought of him?

"Put on a happy face," he muttered to himself the catchphrase he said to Emily so often.

Emily thought he was talking to her. "My happy face puts itself on when I'm with Nicola."

Great. Now he really felt like an ogre.

Angela, her fair skin flushed with heat, waved to him from the kitchen and called Emily to come and help her.

"I'll get you a beer," Nate said and ushered him into the living room where Nicola was inspecting an ornament on the Christmas tree. She wore loose jeans and a thick green sweater. Her hair was combed but that was the extent of it. No makeup. No jewelry except for a flat silver band around her wrist. Aidan could imagine her as a young girl, climbing trees, walking along fences.

"Hi," Aidan said, feeling uncomfortable. This had better not be one of Nate and Angela's matchmaking schemes. They'd be *way* off the mark if it was.

Both hands curling around her wineglass, Nicola nodded.

Nate returned and handed Aidan a tall glass of foamy beer. "Crisis in the kitchen. Angela needs a hand for a few minutes. You can munch on these," he added, setting a dish of mixed nuts on a coffee table made from a large burl. In too much of a hurry to notice the tension, he smiled. "I guess you two can amuse each other for a while."

He went out and in the ensuing quiet the sounds from the kitchen suggested Angela and Emily were having a good time chopping and chatting.

"I was just admiring Nate and Angela's tree," Nicola said finally. "I noticed you don't have one yet. Will you be getting one soon?"

"We don't go in for Christmas decorations much."

"Too bad. Kids like that sort of thing."

There was another awkward silence while Nicola sipped her wine. Aidan took a handful of nuts.

"I wish you'd reconsider and let me continue to look after Emily," she said formally. "I would respect your wishes if you told me what activities are acceptable."

"Even though you think I overreacted to the situation," Aidan said flatly. He took a seat on the oxblood leather sofa against the window.

"So you heard that." Nicola picked up her wineglass from the mantelpiece and crossed the room to sit in one of the matching chairs. "I do think you overreacted. You didn't trust me."

"Don't take it personally," he said. "No one would take as good care of Emily as I would."

"Probably not," she conceded. "But near enough."

"Near enough isn't good enough."

"You lost Charmaine and now you're overcompensating with your daughter."

"Please, spare me the pop psychology." That her words held an element of truth didn't make them any more palatable. He knew he was overcompensating but saw no reason to change. "Better safe than sorry."

"Then tell me," Nicola said, her gaze penetrating, "how is it possible that Charmaine could fall off a cliff when you, who are thoroughly trained in emergency rescue operations, were standing right beside her?"

"If this is your idea of social discourse—" he began, irritated, then stopped abruptly. "Has it not occurred to you that her death is painful for me to talk about?"

"I'm sorry, but I loved Charmaine, too," Nicola said. "Not knowing what happened is awful. Imagine how you'd feel if you hadn't been there and had to rely on secondhand information, especially when the stories are contradictory."

Aidan cradled his beer glass in his hands. He felt the cold seep into his skin the way it had permeated his very soul that day on the mountain. He could tell Nicola wasn't going to give up until she had answers.

"It was snowing heavily," he said at last. "Charmaine had gone into the permanently closed area."

"Why would she do that?" Nicola interrupted. "She was an experienced skier…she'd know the danger involved."

Aidan recalled his shock when he glimpsed her through the blizzard and realized how close to the cliff edge she was. "The rope that fences off the area had broken and was buried under snow. I was there, fixing it. Rich called me on the two-way radio, warning me about where she was headed."

Aidan fell silent, ruminating. It had been a miracle he'd even spotted her through the blizzard, a speck in a dense white swirl of snow. And if he hadn't…. Aidan shuddered to think how much greater the tragedy could have been.

"Go on," Nicola said quietly.

"I skied over to her. We…talked," he said, glossing over things that were none of Nicola's business. "I realized too late the slope was unstable. One second she was standing beside me, the next second the snow she was standing on literally fell away and she was sliding backward, away from me. I was lucky I didn't fall, too. I was standing on a rocky outcropping where the top layer had been blown away. There was no time to reach out and grab her." His hands tightened their grip on his glass as if even now he might grasp hold of her. Save her.

"Witnessing her fall must have been awful." Nicola impulsively reached across and touched his hand. "Did you tell June all this?"

"Of course," he said stiffly. "She believes what she chooses to believe." He glanced down at Nicola's fingers resting on his. Her nails were short, unpolished but well-kept. Her innocent touch held comfort and understanding. Or was that an illusion he'd like to believe?

Nicola noticed he was staring at her hand and tucked it in her lap, her cheeks turning pink. "Did Charmaine say anything before she died that would explain what she was doing there?"

He hesitated before shaking his head, just a fraction of a second, but it was obviously long enough to instill doubt in her voice because she added insistently, "Isn't there anything else you can tell me?"

Frustration surfaced. All these questions. Would Charmaine's death never be forgotten? "What more do you want me to say?"

"I don't know," Nicola said, sighing. "Her death seems so pointless, so incomprehensible. I want to fill in the gaps in my understanding, find some small detail that will give her death meaning."

"It *has* no meaning," he said bluntly. "That's why it's a tragedy."

Nicola studied Aidan's tormented face and began to wish she'd never brought the subject up. He was right; Charmaine's death was hardly dinner party conversation.

Nate returned with the wine bottle and topped up Nicola's glass. Then Angela breezed in from the kitchen carrying a plate of appetizers which she set on the coffee table. She was immaculately dressed, casual but chic with slim gold jewelry adorning her wrists and ears. "Sorry to take so long."

As if someone had waved a magic wand, Aidan's forehead smoothed and his mouth lifted in a smile. "Angela, those look good enough to eat."

He was putting on his "happy face," Nicola thought as she watched him charm his sophisticated sister-in-law into blushing like a schoolgirl. She could understand how Charmaine had fallen in love with him. Any woman would. Any woman susceptible to charm and good looks, that is.

Emily came into the room carrying a very full glass of orange soda, her forehead puckered in concentration. Aidan's eyes followed her until she'd successfully set her glass on the coffee table.

"Please, help yourself to a pakora." Angela offered the plate of spicy vegetable fritters to Nicola and Aidan.

"Mom heard from Marc," Nate told them. "He and Fiona will be back from their honeymoon in Greece next weekend."

Nicola dipped a pakora into the accompanying bowl of sauce. "Marc's your cousin, isn't he?"

Aidan, poker-faced and chewing steadily, nodded. Finally, with effort, he swallowed. "He suffered a spinal injury in the Middle East, but he's recovering."

"I can't wait to see them again," Angela said. "How are the pakoras?"

Nicola bit into her appetizer and encountered hard vegetables inside soggy batter. "Tasty," she conceded, "although they could use a little more cooking."

"You should have seen the first dinner she cooked for me when we were getting back together last summer—completely inedible. Wasn't it, sweetheart?" Nate dropped into a chair and squeezed Angela's hand with a teasing smile. "I almost gave you that divorce you pretended you wanted."

"Brat! I've improved since then." Angela took a

pakora, dipped it in the sauce and took a bite. "Oh, dear," she said after a moment. "I should know better than to experiment on company."

"Luckily her roast chicken is foolproof," Nate said. "I promise you won't starve."

Nicola wiped her fingers on a napkin and turned her attention to Emily who was sitting so quietly among the adults. Wanting to include the child she asked, "Would you like me to put your hair in a French braid?"

"Yes, please," Emily said, her eyes shining. She scooted over to sit on the floor between Nicola's knees.

Nicola got a comb from her purse and started to brush Emily's hair in preparation. She saw Aidan watching her and couldn't help needling him. "I promise you, it's quite safe."

"Having Nicola look after you is like having another auntie, isn't it, Emily?" Angela said.

So Aidan hadn't told Angela and Nate he'd relieved her of baby-sitting duties. Nicola noticed him shift uncomfortably on the leather couch. Well, he deserved to squirm. Being a responsible parent was one thing, but he hadn't even given her a chance. Should she enlighten Angela and Nate or would he?

Before either could speak, Angela asked Nicola, "What did you two do today instead of school?"

Nicola began to weave Emily's fine blond hair into a tight French braid. "We started to go skiing."

"It's good to see Emily's getting out on the mountain," Angela said. "You'll be a ski bunny before you know it," she added to the little girl.

"And it's nice to hear you're loosening up, buddy," Nate said approvingly to his brother. "There's such a thing as being too protective."

"We didn't stay long—" *before Aidan put a stop to their activity* Nicola was going to say until she noticed Emily's shoulders hunched in embarrassment and Aidan looking grim. Whether she agreed with him or not, Emily *was* his daughter and he had a right to decide what she was and wasn't allowed to do. He struck her as a reasonable person, if a bit quick to judge when it came to his daughter. Maybe she should give him the benefit of the doubt that with a little time he'd change his mind.

"There were some kids on the hill who were dangerously out of control so we quit after the first run," she said instead.

"Too bad," Angela said. "Someone ought to teach those kids properly so they're not a danger to themselves and others. You have to wonder where their parents are."

Nicola wrapped a hair tie around Emily's braid and tugged lightly on it. "You're done."

Emily reached up to feel the bumps of her hair at the back and smiled. "Thank you."

Across the coffee table Aidan met her eyes. "Yes," he said quietly. "Thank you."

CHAPTER SIX

NICOLA WAS WATCHING TV with Roy in the family room on Sunday evening. It was a more comfortable space than the living room, with well-worn furniture and a battle-scarred coffee table, and her uncle was an undemanding companion. But Nicola was finding it hard to concentrate on the prime-time movie; she kept wondering who was going to look after Emily tomorrow.

During a commercial break, she turned to Roy. "Aidan didn't call today, did he?"

Roy pressed the mute button on the remote control. "Not that I know of. Were you expecting him to?"

"Not really." Maybe he was finding it hard to back down after taking such drastic action. Or maybe she'd pushed him too hard about Charmaine and he was glad of an excuse to find someone else.

While she was pondering this her aunt came in with several long dresses on hangers draped over her arm. "Stand up," June said. "Let's see what looks good on you."

Reluctantly Nicola rose. "I doubt Charmaine's dresses will fit me. She was at least three inches taller and, well, a lot more buxom."

"Don't worry about that," June said, dismissing her objections. "Whatever you choose I can alter to fit you."

"Would you really want to do that?" Roy interjected.

Ignoring him, June busied herself looking through the individual dresses. "This blue one would go nicely with your coloring. Or do you like the red? Charmaine looked fabulous in this."

Nicola recognized the hot red number Charmaine had written her about, the dress that was cut so low Aidan hadn't been able to take his eyes off her breasts. "Uncle Roy has a point. It'd be a shame to ruin it with alterations."

June clasped the dress to her chest. "I just want to see them worn again. Not on strangers, of course, but you're family, Nic. Please try one on. It would mean so much to me."

What could she do but acquiesce? Once June saw that Nicola couldn't do the clothes justice surely she would drop the idea. But no matter what June wanted, if Nicola didn't feel comfortable she wouldn't wear them.

Nicola took Charmaine's red dress upstairs to her room and removed her own clothes. In the mirror over the dresser she caught sight of herself in her plain cotton bra and quickly drew the evening gown on over her head before she changed her mind. As she'd expected, the bodice hung loosely over her small breasts and the waist bagged down around her hips. The hem, which should have skimmed her ankles, pooled on the carpet.

"Nic, how are you doing?" June called up the stairs. "Do you need any help?"

"No, thanks. It doesn't fit."

"Come down and let me see."

Nicola closed her eyes. "All right." She might as well get it over with. Even June would have to agree it was a hopeless case once she saw the extent of the alterations needed.

Gathering a handful of dress in one hand so she didn't trip over it, Nicola made her way down stairs, holding on to the rail. June waited at the bottom, hands clasped, eyes shining. Nicola realized with a sinking heart that her aunt wasn't seeing her but the long-ago image of her beautiful daughter.

"It's way too big," Nicola said when she reached the bottom. "You don't want to ruin it just for me. I don't care if I go to the ball anyway."

"Don't be silly. Wait here while I get my sewing box." As she moved away the doorbell rang. "Can you answer that, please, dear? I'll be right back."

"But…" Nicola protested, not wanting to open the door to anyone while looking like a little girl who'd gotten into her mother's dress-up box. But June had disappeared and Roy was still relaxing in front of the TV with his allotted one glass of Scotch. Okay, so it was his second glass, but *she* wasn't counting.

The bell rang again.

"Is someone getting that?" Roy called from the depths of his easy chair.

Nicola sighed. "I will."

Aidan stood on the doorstep. He took one look at her and his face, tanned by wind and weather, went pale.

Oh, no. Of all the people she wouldn't have wanted to see her in this dress, Aidan topped the list.

"Is that…?" His throat and jaw were working so hard he couldn't finish the sentence.

"Yes," she replied, knowing exactly what he was asking. "This wasn't my idea. June wants me to wear it to the ball."

"No!" He'd gotten over his immobilizing shock and moved past her into the hall, agitated. "You absolutely cannot wear that dress. It's out of the question."

"You don't have to tell *me* that," she replied, stung. "I know what it looks like on me—"

"What it looks like isn't the problem. It's…it's…" he stuttered. "The dress belonged to *Charmaine*."

Nicola felt awful, both for herself and for him. "I'm sorry. Seeing this dress must bring back painful memories."

"If only you knew." Abruptly he turned away, shoulders bowed.

June came into the hall with a soft tapping of her leather flats on the polished tiles and a large floral patterned sewing box in hand. "We'll have Cinderella ready for the ball in no time," she said gaily. She stopped short when she saw Aidan. "Hello, Aidan. Don't you think Nicola will look lovely in this gown of Charmaine's?"

Nicola groaned inwardly. Was her aunt really so obtuse?

"Surely Nicola has a dress of her own she can wear," he said coldly.

"She didn't pack anything suitable. But if you object…" She let her words trail away, as if daring him to do exactly that.

"If I did, would it do any good?" he demanded.

"I only want to cherish Charmaine's memory," June replied with dignity. "Unlike *some* people."

"What exactly are you accusing me of?" Aidan said. "I remember Charmaine, too, every single day of my life."

"Stop!" Nicola cried. "Just stop, both of you. Not everything's about Charmaine!"

Aidan and June turned to her with shocked expressions.

"I'm *not* wearing this dress," Nicola added vehemently. "It's not *me*."

She marched up the stairs, her back straight, her head high. Only when she got to her bedroom did her shoulders slump and she sank onto the bed with her face in her hands.

Even dead, her cousin managed to eclipse her. Even dead, Charmaine aroused more love and devotion than Nicola ever would in her lifetime. Jealousy rose in her like bile, flooding her with anger. Not because Aidan and June were being unfair—they couldn't help their feelings—but because she still compared herself to Charmaine and found herself wanting. With jealousy came guilt; she'd loved Charmaine, too.

Getting up she tugged the dress off her shoulders wishing she could as easily strip away the gawky teenager who always stood on the sidelines, overshadowed by her cousin. She stepped out of the dress, leaving a pool of red silk on the floor, and reached for her jeans.

She had one foot in a pant leg when she heard heavy footsteps coming up the stairs. That didn't sound like June and it was unlikely Roy had moved from in front of the TV. Hurriedly she inserted her other leg and drew the jeans on over her hips.

"Nicola." Aidan pushed open the door she'd left ajar.

Her jeans undone, her top bare except for her bra, Nicola froze, too surprised to cover herself.

Aidan was too surprised, apparently, to glance away.

The look in his eyes made her cheeks burn.

Aidan recovered himself first. He spun around and stood with his hands on his hips, eyes cast down. "Sorry, I wasn't thinking. I should have knocked."

Nicola quickly zipped up and scrambled to pull on her sweater. "What do you want?"

"To apologize," he said tightly.

"You just did," she replied, confused. "It's okay."

"I didn't mean about seeing you."

"Of course. The…the dress," she stammered. "I understand."

"Not that, either." He was starting to sound impatient, whether with her or himself, she couldn't have said. "Are you decent?"

Nicola glanced down. Her body was covered from neck to ankles in a bulky fisherman knit sweater and blue jeans. "Yes."

Aidan turned around. Again his gaze ran over her; this time cursory and impersonal. Maybe she'd imagined that hint of dawning admiration earlier. It was humiliating to realize how much she wanted him to see her as a desirable female. How much she liked the idea that the man who'd loved Charmaine would look at *her* that way.

These ignoble thoughts flicked through her mind in the time it took to shake her hair into place. Men didn't think of her like that. Not men like Aidan Wilde who could have any woman he desired. It wasn't Charmaine's fault she'd been beautiful and Nicola was plain. Besides, beauty wasn't everything. Nicola had talent and determination. She would have to be satisfied with that. She *was* satisfied.

By the time she was herself again she'd repressed both the yearning for a sexual spark between her and Aidan, and the glory and the shame of trying to usurp her dead cousin.

"What, then," she was able to ask calmly, "do you have to apologize for?"

To her surprise, he appeared uncomfortable. "For getting angry at you the other day. You weren't to know that Emily isn't allowed to go on the mountain. I assumed, perhaps unfairly, that June would fill you in on the details we worked out long ago. I'm sorry."

"Apology accepted." Nicola resisted the impulse to argue the correctness of his decision. He was Emily's father, after all. "Where *is* Emily?"

"She's waiting in the car. I told her I'd only be a

moment." He glanced at his watch. "She'll be wondering what's happened to me."

"Say 'hi' to her for me." Nicola couldn't keep a wistful note from entering her voice. She hadn't known Emily long but the little girl had already wriggled into her heart.

Aidan thrust both hands into his pockets of his open jacket to the jangling sound of car keys and coins. "I didn't come all the way over here just to apologize. I also wanted to ask if you would consider looking after Emily again."

Joy leaped in Nicola's chest but she made herself cross her arms and say sternly, "Couldn't find anyone else, is that it?"

"I could, but…" He looked directly at her. "Emily likes you. I like you. Will you come back? Please?"

The sincerity of his appeal was as devastating as the intensity of his gaze. She could only say, "I'd be glad to."

"Thank you." He reached out to tuck a strand of hair behind her ear and as he did so, his fingers grazed her cheek. Softly he added, "You deserve a gown of your own, Cinderella."

Nicola went completely still, fighting the urge to throw herself into his arms and press her face into the warmth of his fine wool shirt. When she felt herself losing the battle she turned to her bedside table and reached for an envelope of photos. Nervously she shuffled through them.

"Did I show you the pictures I took the other day?" she asked. "There are some great ones of Emily."

"Bring them over tomorrow and I'll look at them." And then he was drawing away, murmuring goodbye.

From the landing she watched him go downstairs and let himself out. Only then did her heart rate slow to normal. Good Lord, what was happening to her? She couldn't be falling for Aidan. She'd end up making a fool of herself.

NICOLA'S GOING TO TAKE YOU to school tomorrow," Aidan told Emily as he climbed into his vehicle.

"Goody!" Emily sang out from the back seat. "Thank you, Daddy."

"Thank Nicola," he said, backing out onto the snowy road. "Let's get home. It's late and we've both got to be up early tomorrow."

He drove carefully down the icy hill toward the highway, relieved that he and Nicola had been able to put the discord behind them. He liked her; she was outspoken and down-to-earth and her shy smile was oddly appealing. Best of all, she didn't eye him up like a big slice of chocolate cheesecake, a refreshing contrast to some other women of his acquaintance. No, with Nicola he needn't fear getting himself in some messy entanglement from which he'd have to eventually extricate himself.

Why, she was almost like one of the guys in the locker room at base station. Mind you, she was anything but boyish underneath all those layers of clothing. He'd been pleasantly surprised by her small neat curves.

If only he hadn't seen her in the dress Charmaine had worn to the Christmas Ball the year before she died. His hands gripped the wheel tighter remembering how he'd caught her kissing her old boyfriend Rich at the back of the hall. Rich had smirked; Charmaine had teased him about being jealous; Aidan had seen red.

Which was the real reason he'd hated seeing Nicola in that scarlet dress. But how could he tell her that when she seemed as devoted to the idea of Charmaine's perfection as June?

His emotions were still ruled by Charmaine, he thought as he turned off the highway. He knew he needed to move on but it wasn't as simple as getting over the grief of her loss.

"Look at the Christmas lights, Daddy!" Emily exclaimed, pointing to a colorful display of Santa and his reindeer on a snow-covered front lawn. "Rudolf's nose is blinking."

"That's so Santa can find his way on Christmas

Eve." Aidan smiled at his daughter in the rearview mirror. "What do you want for Christmas?"

"I want a doll house, a puppy like my friend Ashley's, a Magic Lantern, and—"

"What's a Magic Lantern?"

"*You* know," she said impatiently. "It's on TV. It lights up and shows pictures that spin around."

"Oh, that." Aidan didn't have a clue what she was talking about but clearly Emily had given the matter of Christmas presents plenty of thought. "What else?"

"A mommy," Emily stated confidently, as if satisfaction was guaranteed.

Aidan frowned and checked the mirror again. Emily's gaze was fixed on the passing show of Christmas lights that had gone up over the weekend.

"Did you say 'a mommy'?" he asked.

She nodded hopefully at his reflection. "Can I, please?"

"I can't go out and *buy* you a mommy," he said, trying to turn it into a joke. "You don't wrap a mommy up and put her under the tree."

Emily giggled. "You could put a bow on her head."

"Seriously, Em, you know I can't give you a mommy." He'd explained this when at the age of three she found out all the other kids in play school had mommies and she wanted to know why she didn't.

"You could fall in love and get married like Lady and The Tramp," Emily suggested.

"You want a dog for a mother?" he said humorously. "And puppies for brothers and sisters?"

"Da-ddy." She laughed but her tone indicated she was getting a bit cross. "You're being silly."

"Sorry." He pulled into their driveway and parked. "We're home. What do you say we have some hot chocolate before bed?"

"Okay." She had trouble undoing her seat belt but when Aidan went to help her she pushed him away. "I can do it."

Aidan forced himself to be patient and a moment later was rewarded by Emily's satisfied grin as the catch opened with a click. She's growing up, he thought with a bittersweet pang as he followed her up the walk to the front door.

A few inches of snow had fallen since they'd left home that afternoon and their footsteps showed dark against the snow-covered gravel path. The icicles hanging from the corners of the gabled roof had grown another inch. Aidan unlocked the front door and they went inside.

In the living room, embers glowed behind the glass front of the air-tight. "Go get your pajamas on, honey, while I stoke up the fire."

Emily trotted off obediently. Aidan opened the

fireplace door and threw in a couple of small logs.
They burst into flame, illuminating Charmaine's
crystal figurines with a rich yellow glow.

Suddenly he was angry at himself for allowing
Charmaine to rule his home in death as she had in
life. In every other area of his world he took charge,
made decisions and acted upon them. So why wasn't
he able to do something as simple as get rid of these
damn knickknacks?

He seized the ballerina in her pale-pink tutu and
turned it over in his hand. It was delicate, beautiful…and useless. Rage filled him as he thought of
the hours he spent every month wiping these dust
collectors. He went to put it back on the mantel and
it slipped from his hand to shatter on the stone hearth.

Aidan stared at the fragments, still hearing the sound
of breaking crystal. Like bone on rock. There was a
roaring in his ears and an icy wind swirled around him.

Emily ran into the room, her plastic pajama feet
tapping lightly on the floorboards. "What happened?" She saw the broken ballerina and stopped
dead. With a gasp, she covered her open mouth with
her hand and stared at Aidan with wide eyes. "It was
Mommy's. We're supposed to protect it."

"I couldn't. It was an accident." His voice didn't
sound like his own. Then with a blink he came to
himself. He held out a warning hand to Emily.

"Don't come near in case you cut yourself. I'll get a dustpan and sweep this up."

Oddly enough as he cleared away the pieces he began to feel curiously light. "It's okay," he said calmly, as much to himself as to Emily. "The world hasn't ended. The sky won't fall in."

He disposed of the debris and found a large cardboard box in the garage. "Get those newspapers," he told Emily, pointing to the stack by his armchair. "We're going to pack all these fragile things away so we don't have to worry about them anymore."

She ran to get the newspapers. "Are we going to throw them away?"

"No, just store them. You might want them when you're older." He crouched and took her hands to look directly into her eyes. "But if you decide you don't, you can give them away, or sell them, or do whatever you want with them, okay? You don't have to hang on to the past."

"Not even Mommy's?" she asked anxiously. His present actions went against everything he'd told her previously.

Aidan reached for another figurine, the unicorn. *"This—"* he held it up—isn't your mother. It's a *thing* she bought." Why hadn't he seen that before? Carefully he wrapped the ornament in a sheet of newspaper and placed it in the box.

"Are we going to put every single one away?" Emily lifted a crystal dog down and cradled it to her chest. "I like the doggy."

"You can keep that in your room," he said, to her delight. "We'll pick out something new to put on the mantelpiece."

"Can I help choose?" Emily asked excitedly.

"Absolutely. I will need someone with your discerning taste to help decide what looks good."

"Nicola could help, too," Emily suggested. "She has dis…dis… What you said."

"How do you know Nicola has discerning taste when you don't even know what it means?" Aidan teased.

"If it's good then Nicola has it." Emily defended her new friend stoutly. "She showed me a picture of her 'partment in Australia and it looked really pretty."

"Pretty like this?" Aidan asked doubtfully, waving a hand to encompass the room and the expensive elegance that defined Charmaine's preferences.

"No. She had lots of old stuff. But it looked nice."

"Antiques?" He glanced at Charmaine's prize find, a Queen Anne side table.

"Not like that." Emily screwed up her face in an effort to describe what she'd seen. "Pretty teapots and wooden things, lots of plants and comfy chairs."

It sounded just the sort of thing Aidan would like.

But he knew better than to let a woman help deco-rate. That's how Charmaine had turned his place into hers before they were even married. First she'd bought him the side table, then a chair. From there to picking out a china pattern had seemed only a short step. Nicola seemed safe enough but a guy couldn't be too careful.

He ruffled his daughter's hair. "We'll do a fine job on our own."

CHAPTER SEVEN

NICOLA DROPPED EMILY OFF at school the next day and went to the library. Not surprisingly, Charmaine's death wasn't featured in the Whistler tourist newspapers. The librarian directed Nicola instead to microfiche archives of the *Vancouver Sun*. Nicola skimmed through the December and January issues from six years ago hoping to discover the facts about Charmaine's death.

Her cousin's photo was prominently displayed on the front page of the paper the day after the tragedy. An inset photo showed a somber Aidan holding Emily wrapped in a baby blanket. Nicola stared at the photograph for a long time, her heart hurting at the grief and shock so apparent in his grainy black-and-white image.

The accompanying story was disappointingly low on solid information, basically relaying the story as Aidan had told it to her—Charmaine had headed up the mountain during a blizzard on the afternoon of

Christmas Eve. Once there, it was speculated, she'd been disoriented by the driving snow, leading her to enter the permanently closed area and go too close to the cliff. Aidan, alerted on two-way radio by another member of the ski patrol, caught up with her and tried to convince her to go back to the chairlift. Before she could, the snow slipped, taking her with it over the cliff.

Nicola turned to an account of the inquest. The coroner had acquitted Aidan of any wrongdoing and brought in a verdict of death by misadventure. In the process other information was revealed, things that had no apparent bearing on the case. Nicola was shocked and disturbed by reports that Charmaine had visited a Vancouver psychiatrist in the weeks before her death, something neither June nor Aidan had mentioned. There was also speculation about Aidan and Charmaine's alleged marital problems which Aidan responded to with "no comment" and June denied categorically.

June tended to see Charmaine through rose-colored glasses, Nicola mused. On the other hand, she'd always been close to her daughter and could reasonably be expected to know about such things. Certainly Charmaine's letters had given no hint of problems between her and Aidan.

Nicola turned off the microfiche reader and sat

back in her chair, frustrated. Not only were her basic questions still unanswered, she'd thought of a whole new set. If the newspaper reports were true, why was Charmaine seeing a psychiatrist? *Were* Charmaine and Aidan having marital problems? And, Nicola wondered again, what had Charmaine been doing on the mountain in the first place?

By the time Nicola finished at the library and had a late lunch in the Village she had to go straight to the school to pick up Emily. All the way home Emily chattered about the changes that were happening at her house.

"Daddy and me put away all the pretty crystal figurines. We're going to find something new to put on the mantelpiece," the little girl told Nicola. "It'll be like a makeover."

Nicola smiled at Emily's enthusiasm. "What brought all this on?"

"Daddy says it's not right to live in the past." Having delivered this pronouncement Emily's attention was diverted by an extravagant Christmas display and the conversation turned to speculation about how reindeer were able to balance on the steep shingled roof.

Nicola soon discovered that as well as removing the figurines Aidan had also taken down the dusty lace curtains and replaced the antique side table with a sturdy oak one. The French walnut settee was gone, too, leaving a yawning gap between Aidan's recliner and the love seat.

Whatever emotions had gripped Aidan last night must have been powerful. Had seeing his dead wife's dress played a part in stripping away all traces of Charmaine? And if so, what did that mean? Not quite all traces, she amended; her cousin's portrait still held pride of place above the mantel.

Nicola sniffed the air, aware that something was missing. The house wasn't filled with the usual savory aromas. "Didn't your dad make dinner?"

"He got up too late this morning to put the chicken in the slow cooker," Emily informed her.

"Let's surprise him and make dinner ourselves," Nicola suggested and Emily nodded enthusiastically.

Stifling a yawn, Aidan sat at a table in the bump room at the end of his shift and ran his gaze over his completed résumé. Getting rid of Charmaine's things had stirred up painful memories but the feeling of moving on had cemented his decision to apply for the assistant manager's job. Between staying up late to type his application and tossing and turning over the past, he hadn't gotten much sleep the previous night. Before he handed in his application to Human Resources he wanted to check it in case he'd missed something.

Frederik laid out a hand of solitaire to pass the time until he could meet Liz after she closed her yarn shop for the day. "Don't worry. In your case the application is just a formality. You're the best skier on the mountain and you've got everyone's respect."

"Rich is senior to me by two years," Aidan said. "He has just as good a chance of getting the job as I do."

Christy, on her way back to dispatch with a cup of coffee, paused. "I heard they want to make a quick decision and appoint someone before Christmas."

"Why is that?" Frederik asked, laying a black Queen on a red King.

Aidan's expression turned grim. "Bob's been having chest pains. He went into hospital on the weekend for more tests. He wants to stop working as soon as possible."

The door banged open and Rich came in, stamping his snowy boots on the mat. He passed behind Aidan and peered over his shoulder. "I dropped my application off on my way in." His mouth twisted as he gave Aidan a friendly thump on the back. "May the best man win."

"Good luck," Aidan said in return and then glanced at his watch. Emily would be at the window, searching for his lights in the dark. He slid his form into a manila envelope and pushed back from the table. "See you all tomorrow."

"Wait a sec," Christy said. "Are you going to the Christmas Ball?"

"I don't usually." He'd gone to enough parties with Charmaine to last a lifetime. *She* had a ball; *he* watched her flirt with every ski bum in Whistler.

Christy glanced over at the other two men. Frederik was engrossed in his card game. Rich wasn't looking their way but he was stirring his coffee very slowly, his head tilted slightly toward them the better to eavesdrop on their conversation. She turned back to Aidan and finished quickly, "If you don't have a date I was wondering if you'd like to go with me."

"I appreciate the offer but…" He thought fast, racking his brain for a suitable excuse. "Uh, I'm already going with someone."

"Really—who?" Christy asked.

Rich sipped his coffee and studied Aidan with open curiosity, abandoning any pretence that he was minding his own business. Frederik glanced up from his cards.

"Nicola. Yeah, that's it. Charmaine's cousin who's visiting and baby-sitting Emily temporarily. She doesn't know anyone else in town," he added, just in case anyone tried to manufacture a romance out of nothing. Now that he thought of it, Nicola would be the perfect date—companionable and fun, and not in town long enough to expect a relationship to develop.

"I don't think I've met Nicola," Rich said. "Is she a knockout like Charmaine was?"

"She's attractive…in an understated way," Aidan replied. "She's got a great personality."

"Bring her up the mountain and introduce her to us," Rich suggested.

"She's busy taking care of Emily," Aidan said, instinctively feeling he didn't want Rich and Nicola to meet. He turned back to Christy. "Steve's looking for someone to go with," he said, referring to a volunteer member of ski patrol.

"I don't know," Christy said. "Steve's nice but he's a bit young for me."

"I'll go with you," Rich volunteered.

Christy opened her mouth then shut it again as the color rose in her cheeks.

Time to exit. Aidan picked up his gloves and the envelope and backed away. "Catch you folks later."

Aidan dropped off his application and headed for the Land Cruiser. As he drove out of the parking lot he considered stopping for a pizza to take home but that would only delay him longer. There must be something in the freezer he could heat up for dinner.

Emily was waiting at the door when he arrived,

letting in the cold air and letting out a delectable aroma of chicken and tomato sauce.

"Have you suddenly learned how to cook?" he teased her, taking off his coat and removing his boots.

"Nicola made chicken catchy dory," Emily told him.

Nicola appeared in the hall, dwarfed by his big barbecuing apron. "Chicken cacciatore. I hope you don't mind."

"On the contrary, I'm grateful." No, Nicola wasn't a knockout but her gamine face held a certain appeal. "Hang on, you've got a speck of tomato sauce." He removed it with his thumb. "Got it."

Nicola checked herself in the hall mirror, scrubbing at her small pointed chin. Her cheeks were flushed, probably with heat from the stove.

Aidan moved into the living room where the fire blazed and table lamps gave the room a glow. He'd forgotten how nice it was to come home to a warm house with a woman waiting for him.

"Sorry I'm late," he said. "The assistant patrol manager's position is coming vacant and I stopped off to file an application."

"Assistant manager," she repeated, eyebrows raised. "That sounds impressive."

"I really want the job," he admitted. "I'm ready

for more responsibility and frankly, I wouldn't mind the increase in pay, either."

"What are your chances?" Nicola asked.

"I'm not the most senior patroller but I'm more than capable of doing the job." He sniffed the air appreciatively. "How long before dinner's ready?"

Nicola untied the apron. "The chicken is ready now. All you have to do is boil the spaghetti."

"Stay and eat with us." Aidan was surprised at how much he wanted her to. Until now Emily had always been enough company.

"June is expecting me home," she said uncertainly.

"*Please* stay, Nicola," Emily chimed in as if her presence was desperately important. "You've *got* to."

Aidan sensed her waver at his daughter's request and pointed to the hall phone. "Call June and tell her you'll be late. I'll open a bottle of wine."

"I guess I could," she said, but he thought she was pleased at the invitation.

Afterward, Aidan made her stay for coffee. They sat side by side on the love seat, going through her photos while Emily had a bath. The saggy cushions threw them into close contact and Aidan wondered if he ought to move the settee back in from the garage until he found a replacement.

"You can have this," she said, handing him a picture of Emily in front of the fire. "I took that the first day."

"She's usually so solemn in photos but you really captured her cheeky expression," he said. "You're good."

"It's nothing." Nicola gathered the rest of the pictures and put them back into the envelope.

Aidan hesitated, feeling unusually nervous. "I want to ask you something."

"Will you do me a favor?" she asked.

They'd spoken at the same time. "Ladies first."

"No, really," she said quickly. "You go first."

"Okay." He swallowed, smiled and finally said, "Will you come with me to the Christmas Ball?"

Surprise flickered over her face, followed by a shimmer of pleasure. "Are you asking me as your date?"

Suddenly he was aware of how close they were sitting, of her upturned face and gold-flecked amber eyes. What could he say to her—another woman invited me and I used you to get out of going with her? He'd look like a complete jerk. He *was* a jerk.

Keeping his reply light, he said, "What else?"

A smile lit her face and for a moment he forgot he felt like a heel and simply thought about how pretty she was in a wholesome, fresh-scrubbed way. Then just as suddenly the spark died in Nicola's eyes.

"I'd already decided not to go," she said. "I don't

want to wear a dress of Charmaine's and it doesn't make sense to buy an expensive gown I'll never use again."

"The ball will be fun," he said persuasively. "Even if you don't wear the dress again at least you'll have had one night out of it. Come on, what do you say?"

"Well…" She shrugged, beaming helplessly. "Okay."

"Great," he said, smiling. "Now, what was it you wanted to ask me?"

Her smile faded again. "This might seem like a bit of a downer after the ball but… Will you take me up the mountain and show me the spot where Charmaine fell?"

Aidan swallowed. "Why would you want to see that?"

"I just do," she said stubbornly. "If I have to I'll go up there myself and try to find it."

Aidan suddenly felt very weary. "No, I'll show you. But choose a day when June can look after Emily because we'll have to leave before dawn."

The mountain was shrouded in darkness when Nicola arrived at the ski-patrol base station two days later with Aidan. June was spending the day at home stuffing envelopes so she'd volunteered to care for Emily.

Nicola double-checked her supply of film canisters beneath the outside light over the bump room
door. The chairlifts weren't yet running and a muffled boom from higher up the mountain gave evidence the avalanche patrol was on the job.

Aidan sat astride the snowmobile waiting for her,
skis strapped to the machine, his breath condensing
in puffs of white in the frigid air.

With her Nikon SLR and Canon digital cameras
strung over her down jacket she climbed on behind.
Aidan turned the key in the ignition and the motor's
roar rent the predawn darkness.

The throb of the engine was thrilling. Nicola
pushed her cameras to either side and put her arms
around Aidan's waist. Through his bulky jacket she
could feel the tension and power in his body. Contact felt vaguely illicit, her unease a reminder that
even though he'd asked her to the ball he could never
really be hers while his heart belonged to Charmaine.
For her part, she felt guilty even thinking about wanting Aidan. The fact that her cousin was dead and buried didn't seem to make any difference.

Aidan steered the snowmobile away from the base
station and up the road that wound around the mountain just inside the ski area boundary. Nicola inched
forward on the seat and leaned against Aidan's broad
back, pressing her face sideways. She saw the pass-

ing scenery in frames; a Sno-Cat tractor grooming a distant slope, its headlights beaming through the dark ahead of the plow; a fir tree starkly black against the white snow, the thin lines of the distant chairlift cables strung against yet more white. The very air smelled white. Cold and white. Aidan's warmth seeped through fleece and Gore-Tex to warm her cheek.

They crested the mountain peak, over seven thousand feet above sea level, just as the sky was beginning to lighten. Aidan slowed the snowmobile to a halt and cut the engine. Nicola relinquished her hold on him and angled her leg over the seat to slide off the machine.

By mutual silent consent they turned to the east toward the seemingly endless snowy peaks and an opal sky that glowed with fiery colors as the sun climbed over the coastal mountains. Mesmerized, Nicola couldn't bring herself to break the spell by raising her camera. Gradually, gray sky lightened to blue, black trees to dark green. Beside her, Aidan's charcoal hair turned a rich chestnut-brown and his colorless cheeks took on a ruddy hue.

Then a piercing beam of direct sunlight had them reaching for their sunglasses and galvanizing them into motion.

A post had been erected at the peak with signs pointing out landmarks in different directions—

Blackcomb, Singing Pass, Black Tusk… Nicola walked around it, snapping photos.

She located southwest in relation to the sun and pointed across the sea. "Sydney lies in that direction."

Aidan squinted along her arm, one hand resting casually on her shoulder. "I think I see the opera house."

Nicola felt his warm breath on her cheek and the sensual weight of his hand. Did he know how her heartbeat quickened when he was close? Would he avoid these casual intimacies if he did…or would he go further?

Uncomfortable with the direction of her thoughts she moved out of range of contact and raised her camera to take his photo.

"You hide behind your camera," he observed.

"No, I don't." She turned away and snapped a few more pictures.

"Denying a thing exists doesn't make it go away," he persisted. "You use that camera the way you use baggy clothes. Are you afraid a man will be attracted to you?"

How could he know what it was like to be a plain Jane who elicited minimal interest from the opposite sex? If she didn't try then she hadn't failed, had she?

She raised her chin and met his gaze. "Are you saying you're attracted to me?"

"What if I was?" he said, calling her bluff.

Nicola swallowed. "I guess you'd do something about it."

For a moment she thought he might kiss her. Then he jammed one gloved hand into the palm of the other and glanced away. Disappointment stabbed her even though she hadn't really expected him to admit to an attraction. Their "date" for the Christmas Ball was probably no more than kindness on his part. Fine. She liked that he was a kind person.

She put her camera away and snapped the leather case shut. "Where's the permanently closed area?"

Aidan's eyes weren't visible behind his mirrored glasses but his mouth settled into a grim line that couldn't be misinterpreted. He might have agreed to take her to the site where Charmaine died but he didn't like it. "Behind the peak. We'll ski the rest of the way."

The closeness brought by sharing the sunrise was over. In silence they retrieved the skis strapped to the snowmobile. Nicola stepped into her pair and clamped them into place then slid her hands through the loops of her ski poles.

Aidan skied off behind the peak. Nicola followed. Her short stint on the bunny hill hadn't prepared her for more difficult trails and her rusty skills were tested as she skied in Aidan's path. But before long the sheer exhilaration of skiing fresh powder made her forget the object of their journey.

Then ahead on the right she spotted the rope strung above the slope and the sign warning in bold red letters that this area was permanently closed.

The sign was hard to miss, but in a blizzard, with the rope down, she could see how Charmaine might have skied past it. Why else would Charmaine have left the trail? She knew the rules of the mountain and while she had a rebellious streak, personal safety figured high on her agenda. Nicola couldn't imagine her cousin deliberately putting herself at risk.

Aidan ducked under the rope barrier and skied to the edge of a steep drop-off before stopping. His motionless stance and downcast face made him look as though he was praying. Nicola approached slowly, giving him time. This was obviously difficult for him and she was beginning to wonder if she should have made him go through with it. What would she gain by this ghoulish charade? Perhaps nothing but she knew she wouldn't be satisfied until she had answers to her questions. Or as many as he could give her.

Nicola inched forward on her skis, gingerly approaching the edge of the cliff. The ground sloped steeply for a dozen yards then fell away in a sheer drop. A shudder ran through her. "Is this the spot?" she asked unnecessarily.

He nodded, not looking at her.

"Why did she come up here?" Nicola wondered aloud.

He shrugged, looking uncomfortable as always talking about his wife's death.

"It was snowing heavily, right?" Nicola persisted. "Could she have been lost?"

Aidan turned his gaze on her. "She knew the mountain like the back of her hand."

"You were the only person present when she fell," Nicola said, frustrated. "You *must* know why it happened."

"It was an accident." His voice was devoid of emotion.

"I went to the library and looked up reports of Charmaine's fall," she said. "I'm sorry to dredge up painful memories but they raised questions in my mind."

"Oh?" he said warily.

"Was she really seeing a psychiatrist?"

He glanced away. "You can't believe everything you read in a newspaper."

"What about the suggestions you two weren't getting along?" she probed.

Aidan's head jerked back, his hands clenched at his sides. "I know you were Charmaine's best friend but she was my wife and Emily's mother," he said coldly. "Some things are too personal to discuss."

"Where did she go over? I want to know the exact spot."

He pointed to a place midway along the cliff face. "There, as near as I can identify now."

"Where?" She skied forward, skirting dangerously close to the edge.

"To the right," he said tightly. "Don't go any closer."

She angled her skis perpendicular to the slope and shuffled sideways a few more inches toward the drop-off. Snow crumbled and fell away down the steep slope. For a heartbeat she saw herself flying over the edge and her stomach came into her throat. Lifting her camera she began to rapidly snap photos of the area.

"What are you doing?" he demanded. "Come back."

She heard the tension in his voice and ignored it to inch forward a little more, still shooting. Something impelled her to push herself literally to the edge. "Is this it? Am I in the exact spot?"

"Yes! Come back," he said urgently. *"Now."*

She twisted to face him and shot several photos in quick succession. His fists were clenched around his pole handles, his knees in a crouch, shoulders tense. He was five feet away, skis broadside to the slope, edges dug into the snow. Zooming in, she could see beads of perspiration dotting his forehead even though the temperature was well below zero.

Nicola lowered the camera and put the lens cap on. Enough. She didn't want to torture him and she had no intention of putting herself in danger just to satisfy her curiosity.

But as she started to turn around her skis slipped backwards. Her stomach dropped sickeningly and she jammed her poles into the snow. The spikes held…for a second. Then she began to slide toward the cliff face. Terrified, she screamed, "Aidan!"

Before the word was out of her mouth he'd leaned forward, pole outstretched. She grasped it in both hands and held on for dear life. Aidan backed away up the hill, pulling her out of danger.

He staggered backward, she lurched forward and she fell into his arms. They tightened around her and she clung to him, heart pounding.

"You're okay." He breathed heavily, moisture and warmth fanning her hair and his hold tightened. "You're safe. *Safe.*"

"I'm sorry." She wept, shock making her tremble. "I didn't mean for it to go that far."

She broke off, realizing what she'd said, and that he'd gone very still.

"You did that on purpose?" he demanded, holding her away from him in a painful grip, his gaze so fierce she couldn't look him in the eye. *"You were testing me."*

"No!" Even as she denied it she wondered if subconsciously, she'd been doing just that.

He released her abruptly. "Are you out of your mind? If I hadn't been able to reach you, if the snow had given way as it did with Charmaine, you would have fallen to your death, too!"

"I said I was sorry." She was shaking now as much with delayed fear as with contrition.

His voice unsteady, he went on. "If you knew…if you'd seen what I saw, you wouldn't go near the edge. I'll never forget the look in Charmaine's eyes as she went over the cliff."

The horror of that memory reflected in his haunted gaze shocked her into silence. Nicola moved away to give him space. Aidan seemed to have forgotten she was there. He continued to stare, unseeing, out across the steep drop-off. Slowly she raised her camera, aimed it at his face and clicked the shutter.

Aidan stirred, giving his head a shake. "Are you finished here? Skiers are starting to hit the slopes. Someone might see us and get the bright idea that permanently closed areas aren't out of bounds after all."

Nicola heard a humming motor high above and

glanced up to see the chairlift was now running. She'd learned more than she'd expected, more almost than she wanted to know. Aidan had easily pulled her to safety when she'd been sliding toward the cliff. Why hadn't he done the same for Charmaine?

She started to ski back to the trail, then paused as a thought struck her. "Where was Emily while all this was going on?"

He seemed to freeze. Seconds ticked by while he stared at her without answering, as if he was frantically thinking of a reply. At last he said, "She was safe."

CHAPTER EIGHT

THAT EVENING Nicola sprawled on the couch in June's family room and leafed through the photos she'd taken on the mountain that morning and had developed in the afternoon. June was seated at her rolltop desk, checking credit-card receipts against her monthly statement.

"Aidan took me up Whistler Mountain this morning," Nicola said to open conversation even though her aunt knew perfectly well where she'd been today.

"That's nice," June replied absently, ticking off an entry and setting the receipt on a growing pile to one side.

"He showed me where Charmaine fell." Nicola glanced up from the photos to gauge her aunt's reaction.

June's hands stilled, her shaped and penciled eyebrows rising into her coifed bangs. "Oh?"

"Were you looking after Emily that day?"

June hesitated a moment, then said carefully, "I was for part of the day, yes."

Nicola sat up straighter. "Why did Charmaine go up there in a blizzard?"

"Aidan didn't suggest a reason to you?" June said, overly casual.

"No, did he to you?"

"Nothing sensible." June regarded Nicola over her half-glasses and a small shudder ran across her thin shoulders. "He was raving at the time, out of his mind with shock, saying all sorts of terrible things."

"What kinds of things?" Nicola asked.

"Crazy things. I refuse to even repeat them," June said dismissively. "Charmaine wouldn't harm a hair on that baby's head."

"Did Aidan suggest she would?" Nicola could scarcely credit it.

"I tell you, he wasn't in his right mind."

Nicola tilted her head, watching her aunt through narrowed eyes. "When I asked Aidan where Emily was that day, he said she was 'safe.'"

June glanced sharply at her. "So she was. She was with me."

Nicola tried another tack. "Why was Charmaine seeing a psychiatrist?"

June waved a hand heavy with gold rings set with diamonds. "She had the baby blues, nothing serious. The doctor put her on antidepressants and she was fine."

Thoughtfully, Nicola went back to flipping through the photos. She came across the one of Aidan gazing over the cliff where he last saw Charmaine alive. His face looked haggard, his cheeks drawn, as if he were reliving unimaginable horror and sorrow. Nicola looked closer. There was something else in his expression she couldn't put her finger on….

Roy came into the room with his newspaper and tumbler of Scotch. "Has anyone seen my brown cardigan?"

"I put it in a bag with some other old clothes to take to the Goodwill," June said without looking up. "Have you got any credit-card receipts, dear?"

"But it's my favorite sweater." Roy ignored her question to protest.

Nicola moved closer to the floor lamp to better study the expression on Aidan's photo. Without the filters of flesh and blood and conversation the camera lens sometimes saw a different picture than the naked eye.

Roy surreptitiously poured himself another finger of Scotch. Nicola, catching him out of the corner of her eye, winked.

Turning red, Roy cleared his throat. "If you'll excuse me, I'll go finish my paper. Where's that bag for the Goodwill? I want my cardigan."

"In the closet in the spare room where Nicola's sleeping," June told him with an exasperated sigh. "Don't forget your credit-card receipts."

"Later, dear." Roy held his glass in front of him, out of his wife's line of sight, and hurried from the room.

Nicola turned her attention back to the photo. As she studied it under the light a sickening feeling began to form in her stomach. There *was* another emotion in Aidan's eyes besides horror and grief.

Guilt.

He'd denied pushing Charmaine. She believed him but he was hiding something. What did he have to feel guilty about?

AIDAN WRAPPED HIS HAND around a steaming cup of coffee and clumped across the bump room to gaze out the window at a sky that was pure white with the promise of more snow. This was the best winter in years for skiers, and the worst for people like his mother who traveled back roads to get to home-bound patients or his dad, forced to stop work on building log homes until spring.

Almost a week had passed since he'd taken Nicola up the mountain. At first he'd been angry that she'd tried to test his ability to save her when she went too close to the cliff and started sliding. She'd apologized profusely the next day and assured him she hadn't done it deliberately. He'd believed her in the end, partly because it was unthinkable that anyone would risk their life for such a reason, but mainly because Nicola wasn't manipulative.

The more he got to know her, the more he liked her. But ever since that day he occasionally caught her watching him with a thoughtful expression on her face. She was too intelligent not to realize that if he'd caught her in time there was no reason he couldn't have done the same with Charmaine. He wished he could tell her everything, but as much as he wanted to, he wasn't sure he could trust her with the truth.

"Any cute snow bunnies out there?" Rich said, interrupting Aidan's thoughts.

"I hadn't noticed." Aidan glanced at Rich. He usually wore a confident air but today he seemed more cocky than usual. "What's up?"

"Christy was talking to Sue in HR. They've come up with a shortlist of candidates for Bob's position."

Aidan's eyebrows rose. "And?"

"You and I are both on it. Apparently we'll be interviewed next week."

"They *are* working fast." Aidan glanced over his shoulder. Half a dozen members of the ski patrol were seated around the table, playing cards or drinking coffee. No one was paying them any attention. He glanced back to Rich and lowered his voice. "When Charmaine died, did you talk to anyone about...how she was that day? Or about Emily?"

Rich's gaze hardened. "You know I didn't. Not even the police."

"And I appreciate it." What Charmaine did might not have been the smartest thing, but there was no law against it. *As it turned out.*

"I'm not going to drag it all up again now just to sabotage your chances at the job," Rich went on, eyeing him reproachfully. "Trust works two ways, you know."

Aidan silently acknowledged the rebuke. And yet he hadn't been able to trust Rich not to make out with his wife. The man's loyalty wasn't absolute.

"Why are you so worried about people finding out what really happened?" Rich asked, fishing for information.

Rich didn't know everything and Aidan had no intention of telling him the whole story and giving him more power over him than he already had. It was bad enough that Nicola was snooping around, digging up the past.

Changing the subject, he asked, "So are you taking Christy to the Christmas Ball?"

"You don't have a problem with that, do you?"

"Not if Christy doesn't."

Somewhat mollified, Rich added, "Because I wasn't sure if your date with Charmaine's cousin was a real date or a duty."

Aidan thought about that for a moment. His feelings for Nicola were complicated but he couldn't explain them to himself, much less Rich. "We're friends. That's real enough."

"How come you still don't have a Christmas tree?" Nicola asked Emily the next afternoon.

"Daddy doesn't like Christmas because it's when Mommy died." Emily unzipped the front of her snowsuit and pushed it down, struggling to get her legs free. "We're always the last ones to get a tree and then it's just a skinny baby one."

"That's not right," Nicola said. "Put that snowsuit back on, possum. *We'll* go get a tree."

"Oh, no." Emily shook her head, her blue eyes serious. "Daddy wouldn't like that. He said he might bring one home today."

Frustrated, Nicola said, "Okay, but we can at least hang some evergreens and holly. Let's go outside and see what we can find."

The tall cedar in the backyard was a ready source of fragrant green boughs and Aidan's neighbor let Nicola snip sprigs of holly glistening with deep red berries from a massive tree in his front yard. Emily gathered pinecones from the lower branches of the trees that bordered the two properties and placed them in a wicker basket along with the prickly holly.

Their arms laden, they went back inside. Nicola hung the cedar branches over the doorways and arranged the holly on the mantelpiece. Charmaine's portrait seemed to smile down at the transformation with approval.

"What about Christmas decorations?" Nicola asked.

Emily regarded her blankly.

"Do you have any special candles or ornaments?" Nicola elaborated. "Santas or nativity scenes?"

"There's a box of decorations in the hall closet." Emily ran to open the door and pointed to a small box on the top shelf.

Nicola brought it down and opened the flaps to find a string of colored lights, a few glass baubles and a pale blue and white angel for the top of the tree. "Is this all?"

"There are more boxes of Mommy's stuff in the spare room but I don't know what's in them."

"Let's go find out, shall we?"

Mostly the boxes were full of old clothes, books and odds and ends that had belonged to Charmaine. Aidan was as bad as June, Nicola thought, as she sifted through more items that might have sat on top of Charmaine's vanity table—a crystal perfume bottle, another hand mirror and…oh, the ceramic potpourri container with the pewter lid Nicola had given Charmaine the Christmas before her family moved to Australia. Nicola unscrewed the lid and stirred the dry petals with the tip of her finger. They moved with a papery whisper and from them rose the faint scent of yesterday. Nicola's eyes filled to think her cousin had kept her gift all those years.

"I found something!" came Emily's muffled shout from the other side of the room. She had her head and shoulders in a deep cardboard box.

"What is it?" Nicola set the potpourri container back in the box and hurried over.

Her blond curls ruffled, Emily came up holding a glass ball enclosing a tiny sleigh driven by Santa Claus. She shook it and a blizzard of snowflakes swirled around Santa's red cap. "It's so pretty!"

Nicola turned the little metal key on the bottom and a Christmas carol tinkled from the glass ball. Emily laughed with delight, her eyes shining.

"What else have we got?" Nicola said, setting the ball aside to search the box.

"Wow!" Emily breathed, her eyes wide as they pulled out shiny gold and red ornaments, crystal stars and tiny painted wooden sleighs. There were boxes of silver tinsel, colored bells and lacquered balls painted with old-fashioned images of Santa Claus.

"This is a Christmas treasure chest," Nicola marveled. "It's been sitting here in the spare room all these years."

"Just waiting for us to find it," Emily exclaimed.

Nicola smiled at her innocent enthusiasm. Undoubtedly Aidan knew of the box's existence. Or had he forgotten it, just as he seemed to have forgotten to celebrate Christmas?

They heard the front door open. Here was Aidan now.

"Daddy!" Emily shrieked and ran out of the room. "Daddy, come see what we found."

"What are all these cedar branches doing in here?" Aidan's voice, so seldom raised, rang through the house. "Emily, where did you get that glass ball? Who said you could go into the boxes in the spare room?"

Nicola hurried out to see poor Emily looking bewildered and close to tears. "It was my idea," Nicola informed him. Then, seeing the small spindly tree he'd brought home she felt a surge of outrage on the little girl's behalf. "Do you call that a tree? It's barely large enough to sit on the reception desk at Uncle Roy's office. It certainly can't do justice to all the beautiful ornaments and Christmas decorations you have hidden away."

Aidan curtly told his daughter, "Go to your room."

Emily, her mouth tugged down at the corners, set the globe on the table and ran down the hall.

When she was out of earshot, Aidan turned to Nicola. "Those decorations were Charmaine's," he said harshly. "I don't want any reminders of that Christmas."

"Then give them away and buy new ones," she said, fists jammed on hips. "But don't ruin every Christmas of Emily's young life because you can't face the past."

"I'm not ruining her Christmas," Aidan said. "She gets plenty of presents and all the celebration she needs at her grandparents' homes."

"*You're* the most important person in her life," Nicola told him, frustrated by his refusal to understand. "She needs to celebrate the holiday with *you.*"

"We do celebrate. We have a tree, a small one, perhaps, but it's enough." Aidan removed his coat and boots and put them away in the closet then opened the door to his study and paused on the threshold. "This is *my* house in case you've forgotten and I do things *my* way. Pack up all that junk and put it away."

"Is this how Charmaine would have celebrated Christmas?" Nicola demanded. "Or would she have enjoyed her little girl's delight in the wonder and magic of the season? I wish you could have seen the excitement in Emily's eyes when she saw the snow falling in the glass ball."

Aidan stiffened, his back to Nicola.

"You owe it to her to celebrate Christmas," Nicola went on. "You owe it to Charmaine. Otherwise her death is a continuing tragedy. That's not what Charmaine was about. She was life and love and warmth—"

"Stop!" Aidan turned to face her, gripping the door frame. "All these ornaments and decorations…" One hand threshed the air. "She bought them in the lead up to Emily's first Christmas. Every day I'd come home and Charmaine would have acquired some new treasure. Seeing them is a cruel reminder of the day my family was fractured forever. *That's* why we don't celebrate Christmas in this house."

He went into his study and closed the door.

Nicola stared at the blank wall of wood between her and Aidan. He was literally shutting her out. It didn't matter how much fun they had, how much he seemed to like her, when she got too close to difficult emotions, he closed the door.

She banged on it with her fist in hard hollow thumps, not to gain admittance but to express her displeasure. "Life goes on," she shouted.

"Go away," came his muffled reply.

"*You* have to go on," she countered.

Abruptly the door opened and Aidan stood over her, scowling. "Not if it means reliving the tragedy year after year on what is supposed to be a happy occasion."

Nicola jabbed him in the chest with a finger. "It's in your power to remake the meaning of Christmas for you and Emily. Bring out those decorations and celebrate Charmaine as well as Christmas. Turn the things she so lovingly bought into rituals shared by you and Emily in memory of your wife and her mother."

"Charmaine's Christmas things will be forever tainted for me by what happened," he said. "You have no idea how awful those last days and weeks were for us. No idea."

Nicola crossed her arms and looked him straight in the eye. "Why don't you tell me."

His gaze dropped as he ran a hand through his hair and he was quiet for a long moment. Finally he seemed to arrive at a decision. "You'd better come in and sit down," he said at last. "It's a long story."

Nicola entered the study. Aidan motioned her to the armchair beside the bookshelf and resumed his own seat at his desk.

"Before Emily's birth," he began, "Charmaine anticipated our baby with every joy of an expectant mother. All our hopes for future happiness were pinned on our baby's coming." His mouth quirked painfully. "More than you can imagine."

"What happened?" Nicola leaned forward.

Aidan rubbed a hand over his face, looking weary. "Charmaine suffered from postnatal depression."

"June told me she had the baby blues but that it was nothing serious."

"June looked at her daughter through rose-tinted glasses," he said wearily. "Charmaine had more than the blues. Her depression was real and severe although I didn't realize how bad it was until too late. At first I thought her sleeplessness and mood swings were due to the natural stresses of coping with a new baby. Then one day I came home and found Emily crying hysterically in her crib, her diaper dirty and her sleeper soaking wet, while Charmaine lay on the couch staring blankly into space."

Nicola felt a shiver run over her neck and arms, as though the wind that whistled around the mountain peak had invaded Aidan's cozy home. "Go on."

"I was furious that she'd neglected the baby. She didn't seem to care about anything, not Emily, not my anger," Aidan went on. "When I cooled down I realized Charmaine needed professional help. We were already under tremendous stress because of Emily's spinal abnormality."

"Abnormality?" Nicola repeated, a sinking feeling forming in her stomach. "June mentioned Emily had a minor back problem but that it was nothing to worry about."

Aidan gave a short laugh. "That's June, glossing over imperfection again. Emily was born with spondylocostal dysplasia. Two of her vertebrae are missing and the remaining thoracic vertebrae are each fragmented into three pieces. One rib is missing and others are malformed. The doctors gave us the worst-case scenario—stunted growth and curvature of the spine, pressure on internal organs, heart damage and possible early death due to respiratory complications."

"Oh, that poor child," Nicola murmured, sickened. "She appears so normal."

"Emily has a very mild case, as it turns out," Aidan said. "X-rays taken when she was three showed that her spine is growing straight. Surgery when she's older will correct her rib problems. She's short for her age and always will be but she's within the range of what's considered normal. Functionally she's fine. But right after the birth we expected the worst and it was pretty scary."

"So that's why Charmaine never wrote to me after Emily was born," Nicola mused sadly.

"Quite probably. She became seriously unbalanced at the thought of Emily's uncertain future and her mother's inability to accept anything but a 'perfect' grandchild. Unfortunately Charmaine didn't live long enough to find that out Emily was going to be okay."

"Emily couldn't *be* any more perfect." Nicola wanted to go to the child right that minute and give her a hug for all she'd been through. But she couldn't leave until she knew the whole story. "What happened after you decided Charmaine needed help?"

"I took her to a psychiatrist in Vancouver who made an official diagnosis. She was prescribed medication, given counseling."

"And she was okay after that?"

Aidan was silent for so long, staring into the dark corner of his office that a dreadful sense of foreboding made the hairs stand up on the back of Nicola's neck. "Aidan?"

"Antidepressants typically take up to six weeks to kick in." Despairingly he shrugged. "She died before the medication could help her."

Nicola waited for him to say more. She had the feeling there were still things he wasn't telling her but he looked so drawn and weary she didn't have the heart to probe further. She rose and put a hand on his shoulder, wishing she could do more to comfort him.

"I'm so sorry," she whispered, and left.

Aidan heard the *snick* of the door closing and sighed, thinking of how he'd hurt Emily tonight. How could he make Christmas a treasured ritual when he barely survived the holiday? Christmas was when his life had turned upside down, when all that was good had gone bad.

He thought back to his childhood and the family rituals his mother and father had enshrined. The favorite decorations brought out each year to be lovingly attached to the tree or displayed around the house, the delicious tastes and aromas of Christmas baking. He smiled, remembering how he, Nate and Marc had devoured his mom's shortbread and mince tarts almost as fast as she could pull the trays from the oven. Every year his father had dressed up as Santa Claus, even after they were all old enough to know whose eyes twinkled above the fake white beard. Christmas Eve they bundled up in warm clothes and went around the neighborhood visiting friends and singing carols.

What did they do here on Christmas Eve? Watch some stupid TV cartoon special. Where was the meaning in that?

Aidan sat on in the darkening room, memories of past holidays crowding his mind, comforting in their familiarity. His parents had given his childhood meaning; he should be doing the same for Emily.

He didn't think he could bear listening to the tinkling carols on the snow globe Charmaine had played over and over in the days before she died. But shouldn't he try to endure it for Emily's sake? And as Nicola said, for Charmaine's memory?

He thought about the sapling he'd brought home tonight and was filled with shame. Giving Emily a decent Christmas tree was the least he could do.

Slapping his palms on the desk he pushed himself to his feet and went in search of Emily and Nicola. From the darkened hallway he saw them in the kitchen, side by side at the counter, peeling potatoes for dinner. Their animated faces and their frequent laughter made him pause in the shadows to watch and listen unobserved. At first their conversation made no sense but gradually he recognized the familiar characters of Toad, Rat and Mole from *The Wind in the Willows*. His hardback copy of the book was in the bookshelf and he knew it back to front but he didn't know the story they were acting out now. Nicola was ad-libbing using different voices for each character, becoming increasingly wild and silly, until Emily was helpless with giggles and Nicola was laughing so hard she could barely speak.

He cleared his throat and stepped into the lighted doorway. They glanced up warily, their laughter dying. What kind of monster had he become?

"You're right, that tree is pathetic," he said to Nicola. "Will you two help me pick out a better one?"

Nicola glanced at Emily whose eyes had widened with hope then turned back to him. "What about dinner?"

"That can wait, can't it?" he asked.

"Yes," Nicola said.

"Yippee!" Emily bobbed up and down, unable to contain herself. "*I'll* help you pick out a tree, Daddy."

She clambered down off the chair she was standing on and ran over to him, eager as always to be scooped up in his embrace. Aidan's arms closed around her as he hugged her close. His gaze met Nicola's over Emily's shoulder and he smiled. Once again he had cause to be grateful to her. Her words might be blunt, and sometimes painful, but she told him not what he wanted to hear but what he *needed* to hear.

CHAPTER NINE

SUDDENLY IT WAS an adventure, a break from their usual routine. Instead of dinner in front of the fire and a book or TV, they put on their coats and boots and ventured into the snowy night.

Emily was so excited she could hardly sit still long enough to strap on her seat belt. All the way to the village Nicola encouraged her with flights of imaginative excess that would have put Dr. Seuss to shame. Listening, Aidan smiled to himself. Had he really thought Nicola dull and sensible?

"We'll get the biggest tree in the forest," Nicola said, leaning over the back of her seat to talk to Emily. "A tree so big we'll have to cut a hole in the roof and the angel on top will look as though she's flying among the stars. A tree so big the colored bulbs will be as big as streetlights."

"With ornaments as big as basketballs," Emily exclaimed.

"Bigger," Nicola said. "As big as cars. And the presents underneath will be as big as houses."

"How will you wrap them?" Aidan asked, trying to inject a little common sense into the conversation. Fat white flakes hit the windshield and melted, to be whisked away by the wiper blades.

Emily laughed. "Daddy, don't be silly!"

"Me, silly? What about you two?" He lowered his voice. "Be careful what you say, Nicola. Emily might actually believe we'll get a tree that big."

"Emily's not *th*illy," Nicola replied indignantly with a passable imitation of the girl's lisp. In the back seat, Emily howled with laughter.

Aidan shook his head and heaved a resigned sigh. "'Tis the season to be jolly."

For some reason that set them off again. He gave up and began to chuckle, eventually joining in wholeheartedly. Laughing felt good; he let go of some of the tension that accumulated at this time of year. Talking to Nicola about Charmaine had made him feel less weighed down by the past.

Blazing lights marked the corner lot where the Scouts, bundled in heavy jackets, were selling Christmas trees. Aidan parked and the trio wandered through the rows of cut trees in search of the perfect specimen.

"Brr," Nicola said, tucking up the collar of her jacket. "This is such a switch from Australia."

"It's summer there now, isn't it?" Aidan said. "What will your parents do for Christmas without you?"

"They'll be all right. They always have a barbecue around the pool with Mom's side of the family. I miss them all," she admitted. "But I'm actually very glad to be spending the holiday here in Whistler. I'll never get used to a hot, sunny Christmas. This feels like coming home."

"Do you think you would ever move back to Whistler?"

Her eyebrows rose under her bangs. "I have no plans to, but I wouldn't rule it out. Given the right circumstances, anything's possible."

It wasn't hard to guess what those circumstances might be, Aidan thought. A man or a job. Or maybe, given Nicola's independent nature, just a change of scenery. He didn't like the idea of her leaving after Christmas. She was someone who'd known Charmaine almost as well as he had; that gave them a bond.

"What about this one?" Emily ran up to a tree not much taller than herself.

"Not quite big enough to reach the stars," Aidan told her with a wink at Nicola.

Finding the perfect tree proved to be more difficult than he'd expected with two discriminating females helping him. Some were too tall, some too small, too bushy, too spindly, too lopsided, even too symmetrical.

"It doesn't look real," Nicola said of a tree that could have been used as a model for Christmas cards. "If it's *too* perfect it looks plastic."

"I won't even try to argue with that," he said diplomatically. Emily ran ahead to scout out better trees. Aidan adjusted his steps to walk closer to Nicola.

Snow dusted her blue fleece hat and the shoulders of her down jacket. Looking up into the sky she blinked as snowflakes landed on her eyelashes and melted, sticking her lashes together. Aidan felt a warm feeling spread through him. Nicola was cute and funny and unequivocally genuine.

"There's something I've been meaning to ask you," Aidan said as they moved down another row of conifers. "How would you feel about staying at our house to look after Emily? That way you wouldn't have to drive back and forth."

Nicola's brow creased as she considered his request. "What about driving Emily to school? I can't take June's car full-time."

"I know where I can borrow a car for a couple of weeks."

Nicola still didn't seem sure. "Can I think about it? June might not like me deserting her."

"Of course. Let me know what you decide."

"I found it, Daddy!" Emily yelled from up ahead. "I found the perfectest tree."

She'd found so many before he wasn't expecting this one to be any different but he quickened his pace anyway, with Nicola close behind.

Emily was standing beside a seven-foot Douglas fir, one mittened hand possessively clutching a branch while she bounced on her toes, impatient for them to catch up.

Aidan held the tree out from the wire fence against which it rested and spun it around on its trunk. It *was* the perfect tree, bushy but not too dense, tall but not towering, symmetrical but not uniform. "Emily, I think you've found our tree."

"Well done, Emily," Nicola commended, smiling at her.

Emily threw her arms up and her head back. "Yippee!"

YOU COULD TELL A LOT about a man by the way he tackled tangled Christmas lights, Nicola thought, as she carried mugs of hot chocolate into the living room a short time later. Aidan sat cross-legged on the floor, calmly unsnaring the twisted mass of wires and colored bulbs. Emily was less patient and needed constant convincing that she had to wait until he'd strung the lights before she could hang ornaments.

Nicola set the steaming mugs on the coffee table and went to the window, listening with half an ear to

Aidan telling his daughter tales of his childhood Christmases. Drawing back the curtains with her hand she shaded her eyes from the light and peered into the night. "It doesn't look as though the snow's going to stop any time soon."

Aidan left the lights to join her at the window. "The forecast is only for flurries."

"These are more than flurries," Nicola replied. "I should go while the roads are still passable."

"You can't go now," Emily informed her. "You have to help us decorate. You promised."

Nicola didn't want to leave and not just because the roads were treacherous. She wanted to be part of their Christmas—the glowing fire, the carols playing softly on the CD player, Emily making garlands of colored paper circles. And Aidan, who was standing so close she could almost hear his heart beating.

Meeting his gaze, she said, "I'll stay awhile."

Aidan smiled down at her. "Good."

Suddenly breathing was difficult. She moved away, reflexively reaching for her Nikon. Aidan's gaze follow her motion and her fingers froze, stopping short of picking it up. He was right, she *did* hide behind her camera. But how else to conceal her flustered feelings when he looked at her?

"I'll go see what else I can find in the way of decorations." She fled down the hall to the spare room.

Aidan had agreed to bringing out the big box of tree ornaments but there was another carton of Christmas decorations so far untouched. Nicola sat on the floor and picked through cinnamon-scented candles, a linen tablecloth with a festive motif, napkin rings, candy dishes. There was even a ceramic nativity scene.

At the bottom of the box she found a handmade red felt Christmas stocking with *Emily* embroidered in green and gold. Nicola smoothed her fingers over the soft fabric, imagining Charmaine making it for her baby daughter, and felt the dry crinkle of paper inside. She slipped her hand into the stocking and pulled out several sheets of folded airmail letter paper. How odd.

Nicola opened the letter and knew at a glance that the elegant closely-spaced handwriting belonged to Charmaine. She looked at the date. A shiver ran down her spine.

December 24. The day Charmaine died.

The letter was addressed to Nicola, one she'd written after Emily's birth—and never sent. With trembling hands Nicola began to read.

Dear Nic,
It's the afternoon of Christmas Eve and it's snowing a blizzard. Emily is finally sleeping. I'm sorry I haven't written for so long. I

*haven't been myself lately. Poor Emily's been
impossible today, crying and crying. I wish I
could end her misery.*

"Nicola?" Aidan's voice sounded outside the door.

Without thinking Nicola thrust the letter beneath
the stocking. "Yes?"

He appeared in the doorway. "Are you coming?
I've got the lights on the tree and Emily's champing
at the bit to hang the ornaments, but she doesn't want
to start without you." He paused, noticing the red felt
in her lap. "What's that?"

Nicola's pulse accelerated. "A Christmas stocking Charmaine must have made for Emily. Em would
love it."

Aidan's jaw tightened but he nodded. "Bring it out."

Nicola opened her mouth to tell him about the letter, then abruptly shut it. Producing the letter now
would change the whole tenor and focus of their
evening. This was *her* night with Emily and Aidan,
she thought, feeling a deep resentment that even
now Charmaine might steal the show. Nicola struggled with herself, unwilling to do the wrong thing
out of petty jealousy. This was likely the last com-
munication from his dead wife and Aidan deserved
to see it. On the other hand, Aidan was relaxed and
happy; dredging up reminders of Charmaine might

plunge him into sadness, destroying his newfound desire to make Christmas special for Emily.

"Tell Emily I'll be right there," Nicola said.

Aidan left. She refolded the letter and stuffed it deep in the side pocket of her cargo pants. Since it was addressed to *her*, Nicola, she had a right to read it first. But not tonight.

She went back to the living room where Aidan had set up the tree in front of the window that overlooked the lake. The colored lights twinkled. Emily's beaming face was framed by a long red garland draped around her neck. Nicola was convinced she'd done the right thing in hiding the letter. For now, at least.

"Hurry, Nicola," Emily urged. "Help me put this near the top."

Nicola lifted the end of the garland into place high in the upper boughs, letting the little girl run around the tree, setting it in place. Nicola glanced up and caught Aidan watching her, a warm smile on his face. Awareness of him made her go quiet, but Emily was doing enough talking for the three of them. The air hummed between Nicola and Aidan, their eyes meeting at intervals, their hands brushing occasionally, sparking a glance, a smile, a conscious stepping back.

Was she imagining the chemistry? Had her fantasies taken over her brain, leaving her with no judgment? Was she, as she'd feared, making a fool of herself? She didn't have enough experience with men to know for sure. She found herself glancing at Charmaine's portrait and wondering what *she* would think.

Aidan wasn't making any overt gestures or touching her deliberately yet she thought she sensed in him a mutual attraction. They laughed at Emily's contagious enthusiasm and conferred over whether the tree was "done." Charmaine had collected so many ornaments it was impossible to find room for them all.

Finally Aidan said, "Enough."

"What about the angel, Daddy?" Emily demanded, holding up the fragile glass ornament. "We can't forget the angel."

"*You're* my angel," Aidan said, swinging her into his arms and lifting her up high. "I'm going to put *you* on top of the tree."

Squealing with laughter, Emily guided the angel over the small white bulb clipped to the top branch. The angel glowed and Emily clapped her hands with glee. "She's beautiful."

Aidan set her on the floor and glanced at his watch. "Okay, Miss Muffet. Time for bed."

"Before she goes, you two stand by the tree and I'll take a photo," Nicola said, reaching for her camera.

"Can you set that on a timer so you can be in the picture, too?" Aidan asked.

"Yes, but you don't want me in a family photo."

"Yes we do!" Emily shouted.

Nicola set the camera on the coffee table and focused then hurried to join Aidan and Emily under the tree. With Emily between them, Aidan reached behind his daughter to put his arm around Nicola, his hand settling on her waist. She was so conscious of his touch she almost forgot to smile. Then the flash went and she breathed again.

"I'd better get going." Rising, she hugged Emily. "'Night, possum. See you tomorrow."

"Good—" the little girl yawned "—night."

Nicola packed away her camera and went out to the hall closet for her down jacket.

Aidan helped her into it. "Thanks for tonight."

"I had fun." She glanced down at herself, feeling like the Michelin Man in her bulky jacket. For the first time in a long time she wished she took more care with her clothes.

"I'm going to Vancouver after work tomorrow to do some Christmas shopping," he said. "Come along and you can buy a dress for the ball."

"Okay." She smiled up at him foolishly, all objections to the Christmas Ball vanishing at the prospect of going with Aidan. She'd thought when he asked her he was just being kind; but after tonight, well, it really felt as though they were going on a date.

He smiled back at her. For one crazy moment she thought he was going to kiss her. She'd actually rocked forward onto her toes when he gave his head a shake and stepped back. "Emily'll be waiting for me to tuck her in. Drive carefully."

"Sure." Gripping the handrail, she walked backward down the steps. "See you Saturday."

Dolt, idiot, moron, she berated herself all the way home even though her heart was singing.

He smiled at me.

He thinks of you as the girl next door.

We have chemistry.

Don't let him see how you feel.

AIDAN HADN'T BEEN inside a ladies' clothing store in years. As he followed Nicola through the lingerie section of yet another boutique in Vancouver's Pacific Centre Mall he began to wish he'd let Nicola go off shopping by herself.

The problem was, so far she'd been unable to find a single dress she liked and, left to her own devices, she might not bother continuing. Ahead of him, Nicola plowed doggedly through the racks of lace and satin, looking more like the hunted than the hunter.

Emily, a veteran of many such expeditions with her grandmother, led the way toward the row of evening gowns at the back of the store.

They'd done their Christmas shopping first, Nicola buying presents for her aunt and uncle, and Aidan for his family. By taking turns at going off separately with Emily they'd managed to buy her presents, too. Aidan found the Magic Lantern and gave Nicola a whispered suggestion to choose a paint set and easel, one of the few items June hadn't thought of yet.

As he squeezed between racks of brassieres Aidan remembered why he'd never liked going shopping with Charmaine. There were too many hazards for a big man, especially one carrying a load of shopping bags. At least this exclusive shop didn't have pop music blaring over the speakers.

When he caught up with them Nicola was flipping listlessly through the rack of long dresses. Emily held out a frothy pink number with layers of gauzy folds. "This is pretty."

Nicola, in her regulation bulky sweater, army pants and heavy boots, shook her head firmly. "It's not me."

"What do you think, Daddy?" Emily demanded.

"I agree with Nicola. It's too fussy." Aidan studied her shape, what he could see of it, and her coloring. "You'd look good in blue."

"Blue is my favorite color," Nicola conceded. "If it's the right blue, not too dark."

A petite black-haired saleswoman glided over and smiled at the three of them. "May I be of assistance?"

"I'm looking for an evening dress," Nicola said.

"Something blue," Aidan elaborated. "Nothing frilly."

"But pretty," Emily insisted. "It has to be pretty."

"Of course." The saleswoman sized Nicola up then flicked rapidly through the hangers, picking out dresses in varying shades of blue. "Try these on to start. Through here," she said, leading the way past an alcove with a full-length three-way mirror to the fitting rooms, adding over her shoulder to Aidan. "Please, have a seat."

Aidan retreated to the small couch tucked inside the alcove. Emily sat next to him, perched on the edge as if eagerly awaiting a matinee. A moment later she popped up again and ran to the fitting room. "You have to come out and show us."

Aidan heard only a muffled reply, but it must have been negative because Emily was forced to be firm with her baby-sitter.

"You *must*," the little girl said. "How else will we know if we like it?"

Aidan smiled; from her imperious tone she might have been employing the royal "we." Under Nicola's tutelage his timid daughter had gained confidence. If only Nicola could gain similar self-assurance with regard to her appearance.

She emerged from the fitting room frowning self-consciously and pushing her ruffled hair into place. "I feel like a scarecrow."

Aidan had to admit there was some truth to her assessment, though he would never be so foolish as to say so. The dress fit too loosely on her slender figure and the royal blue was too bright for her delicate ash tones. Trying to think of a tactful way to agree, he lifted his hand wordlessly. Emily simply shook her head.

Nicola retreated to the fitting room and emerged a few minutes later wearing a low-cut dress that pushed her breasts up and had a crotch-high slit up the front.

Nicola stepped in front of the mirror and gasped. "Emily, cover your eyes. This dress is X-rated."

"Very sexy," the saleswoman commended with a beaming smile and a glance at Aidan for confirmation.

Before he could determine the truth of this, much less reply, Nicola had disappeared.

A parade of other unsuitable dresses followed; too tight, too baggy, too dark, too feminine. One, a black sheath, fit well but to Aidan's eyes it lacked sparkle. Nicola would fade into the woodwork wearing it. Maybe that's what she wanted.

"It's no good," she said, two thin lines appearing between her eyes. "I've been through every dress in the store. You'll just have to ask someone else to the ball."

"I don't want someone else," Aidan said. Anyone would think she wanted an excuse not to go. He heard his stomach rumble and glanced at his watch, wondering if he dared suggest they break for dinner.

The saleswoman hurried over, trailing a gown of silvery blue still encased in a long plastic bag. "This one just came in this morning. I think you'll like it."

"All right, but this is the last one," Nicola said with a heavy sigh. "If it's no good, I'll get the black sheath. It fits okay and it's not too 'out there.'"

"What's wrong with standing out from the crowd for a change?" Aidan said.

She rolled her eyes at him and went back to the fitting room.

Aidan, tired of sitting, got up and paced the small area around the mirrors. Emily amused herself by looking through the costume jewelry draped over a nearby display. Aidan was just wondering what was taking Nicola so long when he heard someone go *pssst*.

Turning, he saw her head poking out of the fitting room. "Well?" he said, anxious to finish up.

"It's too risqué!" Nicola wailed.

"I can't tell unless you come out."

Glancing left to right, she took a cautious step outside the cubicle, her arms crossed over her chest, hands gripping her bare shoulders.

What he could see of it, he liked. A lot. The skirt flowed and shimmered on a bias cut from a narrow waist. "Put your arms down."

Slowly she lowered her arms. Aidan's breath caught. The bodice was slashed almost to the waist, revealing tempting curves of firm high breasts. The sleeveless design showed off elegant shoulders and a narrow waist. Nicola looked sophisticated and sexy, like a woman instead of a tomboy. This was a side of her Aidan hadn't had even a hint of until now. Judging by her stunned expression, neither had she.

"You look nice," he said in a massive understatement, sensing that too enthusiastic a response would send her scurrying back to the cubicle.

She turned to examine herself in the three-way mirror. The back scooped below the waist, making this view almost as arousing as the front. "I feel naked."

She had to put that image in his head. A wave of heat swept over him. Aidan loosened the top button of his shirt.

The saleswoman tilted her head, in awe. In hushed tones, she said to Emily, "Your mom is beautiful."

Nicola had been twisting to look at her back. At the saleswoman's words she froze and her gaze met Aidan's. He lifted his shoulders in an imperceptible shrug, as if to say, don't worry about it but he, too, felt slightly uncomfortable.

"The lady thinks Nicola's my mommy!" a delighted Emily lisped in his ear, loud enough for Nicola to hear.

"It's a natural mistake," he said in a low voice. "It doesn't mean anything." To the saleswoman he added, "We'll take the dress."

"I can't wear this," Nicola blurted at the same time. "It's not me."

"It most certainly is you," Aidan protested. "You just won't admit it."

"I'll take the black dress," Nicola said, turning to the saleswoman.

"But—" Aidan began.

The saleswoman glanced from one to the other.

"The black dress," Nicola repeated firmly.

Before Aidan could say another word, she retreated to the fitting room. He heaved a sigh.

The saleswoman exchanged a commiserating glance with him. "The black dress is nice but the silver is special. You make her change her mind."

Aidan lifted his hands helplessly. "I wish I could."

As they walked back through the mall toward the

exit to the parking lot, Aidan said, "That silver dress transformed you. Those bulky clothes you wear are a type of camouflage so no one will know there's a woman in there."

She avoided his gaze, her cheeks flushing. "I'm sensible enough to know I'll never be a beauty like Charmaine."

Her prickly tone hid a touch of wistfulness. A moment's reflection made Aidan wonder what Nicola must have felt always being in the shadow of her older, more beautiful, cousin. He wanted to tell Nicola not to compare herself with Charmaine, that she had abilities his late wife hadn't had and never would have developed. But he couldn't say anything in front of Emily that would reflect badly on Charmaine.

"Oh, I don't know," he said. "In that silver dress you look positively hot."

"You think so?" Her cheeks burned a deeper shade of rose but a light appeared in her eyes.

Emily was walking between them, holding both Aidan's and Nicola's hands, linking the three of them. Her gaze was caught by something in a shop window and she stopped abruptly, bringing them all to a halt. "Look at that Father Christmas!"

The three of them swung as a unit to peer through the shop window at a two-foot-high figurine with

long white hair and beard, dressed in richly orna-
mented robes of peacock blue satin and a cloak of
crimson velvet, carrying a tall curved staff.

"He'd be perfect for your mantelpiece," Nicola
said.

"Can we get him, Daddy?" Emily asked excitedly.

Before he could reply, Nicola said, "Wait here."
She hurried into the store and a minute later, to Aidan's astonishment and Emily's delight, the store
owner was lifting the Father Christmas out of the
window and wrapping him.

"Why did you do that?" Aidan demanded when
Nicola came out bearing the box triumphantly. "We
have a ton of decorations at home."

Nicola hoisted the heavy box higher into her arms
and turned to look at him. "We were talking the other
day about creating rituals. This will be my contribu-
tion. Look on it as symbolic of a new beginning."

A new beginning. Aidan felt a sharp tug in his
chest. Was it possible? He'd never felt ready before,
but in her unassuming way Nicola had opened his
mind up to possibilities no one else had.

He reached for the box. "Let me carry that for
you."

CHAPTER TEN

NICOLA SNEAKED into Charmaine's room while her aunt and uncle were at breakfast and stood in front of the full-length mirror in her new black dress. The Christmas Ball was less than a week away and she badly needed reassurance she'd bought the right outfit.

Unfortunately the mirror didn't provide it. She saw herself all too clearly at times, she thought with a sigh. The black dress would be suitable for the occasion but that was its only virtue. The loose fit concealed her figure and the black washed all the color from her face. The dress was perfect if she wanted to blend in with the furniture.

Face it, it wasn't the dress's fault. She was a plain Jane. There was nothing inherently wrong with her face but also nothing to make her stand out. Two medium-size brown eyes, a sharpish nose and a pointed stubborn chin. The shape and arrangement of facial features turned some people—like Charmaine—into a beauty and others—like her—into ordinary.

What bothered her more than her plain looks was her attitude. Maybe she had no hope of ever attracting Aidan but why did she always opt for the safe, predictable, dull route? The silver dress made her feel sexy and that scared her. Aidan was right about her tendency to hide. Between her baggy clothes and her camera, it was no wonder she felt invisible.

Scooping her hair up she turned from side to side, trying to see herself as attractive. Aidan had said she was hot so she couldn't be completely hopeless. Just once, she'd like to take a chance and make the most of her appearance instead of the least. And while she was being brutally honest, it was also time she stopped blaming Charmaine for her own shortcomings.

Before leaving, Nicola glanced around to make sure everything was positioned exactly as it had been when she came in. She poked her head out of the door to make sure the coast was clear then tiptoed back to her own room. She changed back into her blue jeans, refolded the black dress in tissue and put it back in the shopping bag.

When Nicola went downstairs to breakfast, June was at the table catching up on yesterday's mail. "Oh, good!" she exclaimed, reading the note on a Christmas card. "Mother *is* coming for Christmas."

Roy, obscured by the raised newspaper, extended his hand to feel for his piece of half-eaten toast. "That's nice."

Nicola put a tea bag in a cup and an English muffin in the toaster. "Great. I'd love to see Grammy."

"She's flying into Vancouver at three-thirty," June announced. "Oh, dear. I'll be in a meeting with the caterers for the Christmas Ball. Roy, can you pick her up?"

"The Leafs are playing the Bruins this afternoon," he said, dismayed.

"It's just a hockey game," June replied.

"We're talking about the *Maple Leafs*—"

Nicola cleared her throat. "I'm going to Vancouver today. I'd be happy to pick up Grammy."

"Oh, would you?" June said. "That would be such a help. But where will we put her?"

"I'll pay for her hotel room," Roy suggested.

"I will *not* put my own mother in a hotel," June said indignantly. "Roy, how about clearing out the loft?"

"You can't put an eighty-year-old woman who's had two hip replacements in a third-story loft," Roy said. "And before you suggest Nic sleeps up there remember the banister is wobbly and it's unbearably stuffy."

"What about Charmaine's room?" Nicola suggested.

Roy and June stopped bickering to stare at her.

"Oh, no," June said, shaking her head. "No one's slept there since Charmaine…left."

Roy retreated behind his newspaper, muttering, "Maybe it's time they did."

June got up from the table and paced over to the window. Sparrows were pecking at a lump of suet and seeds on the feeder hanging over the snow-covered deck. "I would have to move all her things, but where would I put them?" She spoke as if to herself. "In some *box?* No, it's out of the question."

"They're just *things,* Auntie June," Nicola said, pouring boiling water over her tea bag. "They're not Charmaine."

"But they *are,*" June insisted, wrapping her arms around herself. "When I look at her hairbrush, I see her brushing her hair. When I smell her perfume, I feel her presence. Sometimes late at night, I go in there when I can't sleep and Charmaine is with me." Turning away, she said, "Oh, you don't understand."

Nicola walked across the room to put her arms around her aunt. June felt small-boned and frail. Sometimes her personality seemed so overpowering Nicola forgot that her aunt wasn't a large woman physically. "Aidan suggested I stay at his house so I can look after Emily. It would make things easier all around."

June went still, then glanced up, blinking away tears. "Would you do that? We want you here, too, you know that. But I can't turn away my mother."

"I understand." Nicola brushed her aunt's hair from her face. "Don't worry. Everything's going to work out."

After breakfast she went back upstairs to pack and tidy the spare room for Grammy. The prospect of staying at Aidan's threw her into a minor panic. She might have a chance with him, she really might, if only she could break out of her old mold. For the first time in her life she cared that she had nothing nice to wear.

Well, she was going shopping, wasn't she? Why do it in half measures?

"Nicola!" June was calling her. "Can you drop me off in Whistler on your way out? Not to hurry you but I have to be there in fifteen minutes."

"Coming!"

Nicola crammed all her bulky, baggy old clothes into a big green garbage bag and thrust it in the closet. Then she swept the film canisters, hair ties, loose change and other bits and pieces from on top of the dresser into her empty suitcase and ran out the door.

Later that afternoon Nicola scanned the passengers emerging from the airport gate for her grandmother. She smiled at the sight of families reunited for the holiday season, greeting each other with hugs and exclamations of delight.

Finally she spotted an elderly woman wearing a purple-and-blue silk scarf between her black wool coat and her thick white hair. She was pulling a carry-on bag and walking with the help of a thin black cane, deep in conversation with a tiny girl of about three carrying a big brown teddy bear. Grammy was just as elegant as June but a lot more approachable. The little girl reminded Nicola how as a child she'd looked to her grandmother for a sympathetic ear to unload her youthful troubles and triumphs. Grammy was probably the only person alive who knew of her mixed feelings toward Charmaine.

The little girl's mother turned around, suddenly panicky, looking for her daughter. "Lisa, honey. Come along."

Grammy gave the girl a smile and a gentle push that sent her skipping back to her mother.

"Grammy!" Nicola went forward to embrace her.

"Nic! I didn't expect to see you here." Grammy's powdered face creased in a smile. "Have you moved back home? June didn't tell me."

"I'm just here for a visit. Let me take that." She extracted the carry-on bag from her grandmother's arthritic fingers and took her arm to steer her toward the baggage claim. "This way. How've you been?"

"I've been well, thank you. Tell me all about Australia, and your mom and dad."

Nicola filled her in on family doings while they waited for Grammy's suitcase to come down the chute. Nic dragged it off the conveyer belt, loaded it onto a trolley and they headed for the exit. From an overcast sky, a light drizzle was falling.

Nicola got back onto the highway leading to the city. The drizzle became heavier and she flipped on the windshield wipers. Peering through the rain-streaked window, she took a left turn onto a sleek span of concrete over the Fraser River. Log booms lined the banks and a tug was slowly pulling a barge upstream through liquid pewter.

"This bridge wasn't here the last time I was," she said. "I hope I can get to the North Shore this way."

"I wouldn't know, I'm afraid." Grammy pulled a comb from her black leather purse and fluffed up her hair. "It's been years since I've been to the coast, not since the Christmas Charmaine died." She sighed. "Poor girl."

Nicola glanced at her quickly, trying to keep an eye on the road as well. "I didn't know you were here then."

"I'd come out to see her new baby. Cute as a

button, in spite of the problems with her spine. I was only here a few days before it all turned to tragedy." Grammy shook her head and clucked, her age-spotted hands smoothing out her wool skirt. "That poor husband of hers, left with a tiny sick baby and June giving him grief for letting Charmaine die."

Nicola changed lanes at the foot of the bridge, squeezing in ahead of a bus. "Do *you* think he had anything to do with her death?"

"Aidan? No. He was as upset as anyone could be. From what I could see he'd been carrying a heavy burden for some time what with the poor sick child and then Charmaine and her problems."

Nicola felt the lingering doubts she hadn't known she'd been harboring dissipate. Grammy believed in Aidan's innocence and Nicola trusted Grammy's judgment more than anyone else she knew. With a mixture of wistfulness and admiration, she said, "He really loved her, didn't he?"

Grammy's hand touched hers where it rested on the gear stick and squeezed lightly. "He was a good husband to her. Have you been getting to know him?"

"Only through Emily." Nicola felt her face grow warm. "Well, he's taking me to the Christmas Ball. But that doesn't mean…you know. We're just friends."

Grammy's blue eyes regarded her with interest. "But you'd like to be more than friends. I suspected when you were a teenager you felt something for him and always thought it a pity Charmaine set her sights on him. You and he were much more suited."

"Do you really think so? I'm so glad even though that was a long time ago. Lately I wonder if I'm just imagining a connection between us. But when I'm with him I feel like…like I've come *home*." It was a relief to speak freely about her feelings for Aidan. And to voice her misgivings. "Am I wrong to want him? Charmaine—"

"Charmaine is gone," Grammy said firmly. "Have you let him know how you feel?"

"Oh, no," Nicola said. "I couldn't tell him *that*."

Grammy smiled gently. "Then maybe you could find a way to show him."

AIDAN MADE A FINAL inspection of the spare room where Nicola was to sleep. He'd vacuumed, dusted and put clean sheets on the bed. Emily had laid out a fresh towel and face cloth on the down coverlet. Worried that it looked too spartan he'd found a bud vase and stuck a sprig of holly in it to put on the dresser.

He'd been surprised but pleased when Nicola had called to say she would like to stay at the house. Belatedly he wondered if he'd been wise in making the offer. Last night she'd been, not *flirtatious* exactly, but more given to making eye contact and less prone to maintaining her personal space. He'd changed as well, he realized even though he had no right to be attracted to her when his past was full of secrets he couldn't share. He was looking forward to having her in his house.

Hearing a knock he wiped his hands on his pants and hurried to the front door. Emily arrived there at the same time, bouncing up and down with excitement. Aidan smiled at her antics. Thank goodness for Emily; she reminded him why Nicola was here and provided a distraction from his unsettling thoughts.

But what about at night, when Emily went to bed?

Nicola looked pink-cheeked and reassuringly ordinary in her bulky down jacket and hiking boots, a shopping bag in her hand. A suitcase sat on the step beside her and Roy's car was backing out of the driveway, snow falling in the glare of the headlights.

Nicola tickled Emily under the arms, making the girl giggle helplessly. "Why are you so bouncy? Did you think I was Santa Claus?"

Aidan reached for her suitcase while she took off her jacket. "Been shopping again?" he said, indicating the glossy black-and-white bag with the vaguely familiar logo.

Switching the bag to her other hand she put it behind her back. "I had some time to kill before picking up my grandmother at the airport."

"I'll show you your room." Emily ran ahead down the hall and stood outside the spare room. "In here. Daddy and me got it ready for you. I gave you my favorite teddy to sleep with."

"You're sweet," Nicola said. "Thanks."

Aidan followed Nicola into the room and placed her suitcase on the end of the bed. "There are spare hangers in the closet. You know where the laundry is and the bathroom. I shower at night so—" He broke off to swallow. *Why was he telling her this?* "Just so you know. If you need anything just ask."

She faced him, her knees pressed against the edge of the bed. "Thanks for making me so welcome."

Suddenly the room seemed too small, the central heating overpowering and Nicola anything but ordinary. Aidan backed away. "Dinner will be ready shortly. Emily, come and set the table. We'll let Nicola get settled."

Aidan retreated to the kitchen. Tired of stews and spaghetti, he'd made a Thai stir-fry with fragrant jasmine rice. He was giving the spicy mixture a final toss in the wok when he heard a sound and glanced up.

"Whatever it is, it smells fantastic," Nicola said, sniffing the air appreciatively.

She was wearing a top Aidan hadn't seen before; a dusky rose-colored knit that clung to her slender curves and skimmed her gently flaring hips. "It's, uh, nothing," he stammered. "We Wildes like to cook."

With tentative steps, she came farther into the room. She seemed nervous, as if aware that her new look heralded a corresponding change in their relationship and she wasn't sure how to handle it. "Can I do anything?"

"Emily was supposed to set the table but she seems to have forgotten. Would you mind?" He nodded to the stack of plates on the counter.

Gingerly, Nicola picked up the fragile china. "You didn't have to get out your best plates for me. I'm a stoneware kind of girl."

"This is all we have, I'm afraid, except for the pasta bowls and the melamine plates Emily uses for after-school snacks."

Aidan called Emily and got her to help carry out the food. In the dining room he found Nicola had moved the pair of red candles from the sideboard to the table.

"I hope you don't mind." Her cheeks glowed in the soft light as she lit them. "I thought it would make dinner more festive."

"Nice idea," he said. "Emily and I don't take time for those special little touches as often as we should."

He'd thought dinner might be awkward but it wasn't, thanks to Emily. His daughter had come out of her shell under Nicola's care. Oh, she'd always been talkative and playful with him but there was something new in Emily's manner; she was…happier.

He met Nicola's eyes across the table and exchanged a smile. Most of the women he dated tried to make friends with Emily but none had succeeded so effortlessly and sincerely as Nicola.

I want a mommy for Christmas.

Nicola would be a good mom; she already loved Emily.

"Daddy?" Emily was tugging on his sleeve.

"Sorry, what was it?" Aidan turned to his little girl.

She looked at him with enormous blue eyes, her hands clasped in prayerful pose beneath her chin. "I said, if I was very, very careful, could I *please* go skiing again."

His hands tensed around his knife and fork. Before he could answer Nicola spoke, her voice calm and reasonable. "If we're both right there with her, and we don't go off the bunny hill, what harm could come to her?"

Aidan looked from one determined female to the other as they waited for his decision. He wasn't comfortable with the idea of his daughter on the mountain but he recognized his fear as irrational. "I'll think about it."

After dinner was over and the kitchen tidy, Aidan stoked the fireplace and they gathered around the coffee table for a game of Go Fish. Aidan handed over card after card in response to Emily and Nicola's requests. They built up an impressive number of pairs compared to his meager collection.

"Poor Daddy," Emily commented complacently as she lay down another pair on top of her haphazardly arranged cards. "You'll never catch up now."

He blamed his poor performance on being distracted by Nicola. Somehow, over the weeks she'd evolved from plain and awkward to the understated attractiveness he'd boasted of to Rich. Seeing her in the silver dress had awoken him, so to speak, but with hindsight the realization had started long before. Head bent, she arranged her pairs in two neat rows. The firelight turned her silky hair into glimmering shades of brown, like sunlight on a creek. She was as subtle as Charmaine was dramatic.

"What's that saying?" he murmured. "Lucky in cards, unlucky in love? Maybe the reverse holds true."

"I hope not, or I'd be out of luck in the love department," Nicola replied.

"Do you have a two?"

"Go fish. You'll make a fine 'catch' for some guy," he said as a pun, checking his cards again in the vain hope he'd overlooked a pair.

Nicola groaned. "That is so lame. Your turn, Em."

"Do you have a thix?" Emily demanded in a lisp. She was clutching her last card.

"I have a *sss*ix," he teased.

"Dad-dy," she said warningly.

"Sorry, honey." He handed over the card.

Triumphantly she laid down her last pair. "I win!"

"Congratulations. The winner is to put on pajamas and report to me for a good-night kiss," Aidan announced.

Emily skipped off to her bedroom. Nicola laid down her two remaining unpaired cards. "Darn, I just missed out."

Aidan shot her a glance. Had she meant that the way it sounded?

Nicola gave him an enigmatic smile. "Emily's probably waiting for you."

Aidan went to tuck his daughter in. When he came back to the living room he found Nicola sitting on the love seat in front of the fire. With a little motion of her head she invited him to join her. For once she wasn't holding her camera like a shield.

"Did Emily go to bed all right?" Nicola asked.

"Fine." The cushion sank beneath his weight, inclining him toward her till his thigh pressed against hers.

Overhead Charmaine looked down on them.

"Did your grandmother arrive okay?" he said after an awkward silence.

"Yes. She's well." Nicola glanced up at Charmaine's portrait and opened her mouth as if to speak then seemed to think better of it.

"Anything wrong?" he asked.

"No." She shook her head and as if to prove it, gave him a shy smile. "I'm sorry I'm not going to see as much of Grammy as I would if I was staying at June and Roy's, but I'm enjoying being here with you and Emily."

"Emily's crazy about you." He fell silent, and another awkward silence ensued.

"Emily tells me you don't ski competitively anymore," Nicola asked at last. "Why is that?"

"After Charmaine died, I was all Emily had. I couldn't risk serious injury or put the necessary time into training."

"Do you miss it?"

"Sometimes."

Aidan left his seat to shift a log in the fire, sending up sparks and a brighter flame. It was one thing to find Nicola attractive and another to know what to do about it. She was different from women he'd been intimate with who'd just been looking for a bit of fun. He sensed Nicola would consider lovemaking to be part of a serious relationshipbut it wasn't fair to get deeply involved with her unless she knew the whole story about Charmaine. But if he told her what really happened, *she* might not want to make love with *him*.

"You're very quiet tonight," Nicola ventured.

"I'm usually by myself after Emily goes to bed," he said gruffly, avoiding her gaze. "Not used to talking."

"Would you prefer I left you alone?"

It would be easier but… "No."

Nicola glanced up at Charmaine's portrait again. "She's a hard act to follow."

He grunted noncommittally and spent another minute needlessly rearranging the logs on the fire.

A hush, like new-fallen snow, settled over the room. Then Nicola said, with a glint of humor in her husky voice, "Do you realize you're directly under the mistletoe?"

He glanced up. Among the cedar boughs and holly was a tiny sprig of white berries. "Where did that come from?"

"I bought it." Without warning, Nicola dropped to the floor beside him and placed her hands on either side of his face. Clumsily she kissed him. He jerked his head at the last minute and her lips landed half off his mouth. The sharp stab of hurt in her eyes was painful.

"I'm sorry," he said. "You caught me by surprise."

"Apparently it's the only way *to* catch you," she replied dryly. With the swiftness of a hermit crab scuttling back inside its shell, she retreated to a corner of the love seat and made herself as small as possible. "Is it just me you're not attracted to, or have you been celibate all these years?"

If Aidan had been drinking coffee he would have choked. As it was his throat closed and for a moment he couldn't speak. When he'd recovered he said, "There've been women, but not many and never for long."

"So it's me," she stated flatly. Her eyes held confusion, frustration and hurt.

"Listen, Nicola, you're a really nice woman—"

"Don't patronize me," she said, frowning. "I know I'm not beautiful or charming. I'm plain and I speak my mind. But there've been times when you've looked at me that I thought… Oh, never mind. I must have been imagining it." She tugged her sweater down at the hem, then up at the neckline. Rising, she was ready to bolt.

"Nicola, wait!"

She paused.

"It's…Charmaine," he said helplessly.

Her eyes fell shut for one pained second then without another word she walked out of the room, head high, back rigid.

Aidan ran a hand roughly through his hair, cursing himself, hating the role he was forced to play. She thought he didn't find her attractive. It wasn't true and she deserved better but he couldn't give it to her, not without destroying the defenses he'd built around him and Emily for six long years.

Nicola kept her back straight all the way to her bedroom, then slumped against the shut door in the dark. She might sag but she was determined not to cry. How humiliating! She'd finally gotten up the courage to wear a sexy top and show him she was interested. All he could say was that she was nice. Nice!

She wasn't nice. She *hated* Charmaine. She'd felt *glad* when she'd read about Aidan's marriage problems because that had given her a glimmer of hope. Obviously those newspaper reporters didn't know what they were talking about. Six years after her death, Aidan was still in love with Charmaine and her cousin still cast a shadow over Nicola's life.

Pushing away from the door she moved restlessly across the room, not wanting to turn on the light and see herself in the mirror. The curtains were open and between the parting clouds the full moon was a cold flat circle surrounded by a halo of light in the black sky. The iced-over lake with its white banks and snow-laden trees glowed palely. The winter landscape was frigid and lifeless.

After the heat of the fireplace, her room felt freezing. A thin layer of ice rimed the corners of the glass pane and condensation fogged her breath. Numbly she pulled off her clothes down to her bra and panties and crawled into bed, pulling the down coverlet up to the tip of her cold nose.

CHAPTER ELEVEN

TEN MINUTES LATER a knock sounded softly. Nicola froze, listening. She heard it again. Shivering, she got out of bed and went to open the door.

Aidan, his dark hair tousled, stood there bare-chested, wearing low-slung pajama bottoms.

"Is everything all right?" she asked.

His gaze dropped to her bare shoulders then lower, to her chilled nipples hardening beneath the black lace of her low-cut bra. Her toes curled against the cold hardwood floor.

"Earlier tonight, you thought I wasn't attracted to you," he said, his voice gravelly. "Not true. I am."

"You are?" The words came out in a whisper.

He nodded, still not touching her though they stood so close her breath ruffled the hairs on his chest. "You're beautiful." His voice dropped a note. "And very desirable."

Nicola tilted her face and he slid his hand through her hair, cupping her head and bringing her to meet

his kiss. Her spirit soared, lifting her beyond fleeting thoughts of resisting. He'd said nothing about
love but what did it matter? Just to experience the
glorious sensation of his mouth on hers was enough.

She felt his other hand settle on her hip, his fingers unbelievably warm on the bare skin above her
bikini panties. As the kiss deepened Nicola felt her
knees grow weak, dragged down by a heavy liquid-
ity in her belly. He drew her closer until the pressure
of his hard flesh against her stomach brought her
back to the reality of what they were doing.

She jerked back. "What about Charmaine?"

His face tightened at the mention of his late wife.
Was it grief or guilt? The light was too dim to make
out his expression. Nicola wished she'd never in-
voked her cousin's name.

"Never mind," she added quickly. "Forget I
asked."

"I can't deny Charmaine is a barrier to me committing to another woman," he said tightly. "I wish
it wasn't so and I know better than to make prom-
ises I can't keep." He dropped his forehead to hers
and shut his eyes. "But God help me, I want you."

That was all she needed to hear. "I'll make you a
bargain," she whispered huskily.

"Anything." His hands moved down her back to
her hips then up, to cup her breasts, his thumbs set-

tling on her nipples, pressing lightly, making it impossible for her to think.

No matter. She knew what she was going to say because she'd thought about it many a night. "I won't plan on a future together if you don't dwell on the past." He started to speak but she pressed a trembling finger against his lips. "All I want are these few weeks while I'm here in Whistler." This wasn't strictly true but if it was all he could handle, so be it.

"Agreed." He glanced at the single bed then put his hands under her bottom and lifted her up.

Startled, she wound her arms around his neck and wrapped her legs around his waist. Nothing like this had ever happened to her. No boyfriend had ever been strong enough, for one thing. Or confident and dashing enough. Nicola threw her head back and laughed for pure joy as Aidan pressed kisses on her face and neck all the way to his bedroom.

Aidan lowered her to the floor, amazed at having made Nicola happy simply by desiring her. He wanted so much to please her. And he would, before this night was over.

Quickly and gently he removed her scanty clothing then his own. Naked, Nicola was small and sleek and feline. Her smile was vulnerable yet trusting. Cupping her hips in his palms he pulled her closer and kissed her again, gently at first, then hungrily. Her hands flat on his chest, she responded, then breathless and trembling she drew back, searching his gaze as if for confirmation that he really did want her.

"I can't believe this is happening," she said.

She was different from other women but how could he let her know that was a *good* thing in his mind? Smooth talk wouldn't impress her and compliments wouldn't woo her. His physical reaction to her body would just have to speak for itself.

"Believe it," he replied gruffly and pulled her onto the bed.

But as hard and hot as he was, when he looked into her eyes as he entered her, his emotional reaction overwhelmed his sensual response. For the first time in years Aidan felt as though he were making love, not having sex. So different to how he'd felt these last few years with Charmaine—

No. He wasn't going to think about Charmaine. The guilt would take over and unless he was very quick… *Damn.* Too late. His body had softened. He stilled, breathing heavily, his skin warm and sticky with perspiration.

"Everything okay?" Nicola asked delicately.

Something in her eyes told him she knew the direction his thoughts had taken. Thinking their lovemaking was over practically before it had begun, Aidan's heart sank.

"We're in *this* moment, no other," Nicola reminded him softly. "If we do nothing more than this, you're still the best lover I've ever had," she added, smiling into his eyes. "You make me feel like a woman."

With Nicola there was no false flattery, nothing phony or manipulative. Lovemaking was a gift, each to the other, not part of some larger agenda. Thoughts of Charmaine receded, guilt was overtaken by his desire to give pleasure to the woman in his arms. Then Nicola began kissing him on his chest, tiny kisses soft as a butterfly wing, and at the same time to move her hips. Her technique wasn't practiced or sophisticated; she probably hadn't had a lot of experience but that didn't matter. What turned him on was the combination of her girlish enthusiasm and womanly appreciation. She was flushed and sexy and had no idea how desirable she looked.

Nicola felt Aidan harden and swell inside her. Thought fragments drifted through her brain, washed to and fro by surges of physical bliss. What should she do with her hands? How could she give him as much pleasure as he was giving her?

Aidan's body was powerful, solid and *sexy*, not tentative and underdeveloped like most of the other men she'd been with. He knew where to touch her, how hard or how gentle. He started slow and deep and when she needed to go faster his rhythm changed instinctively. His earthy murmurings, his stroking and caressing…everything he said and did was designed to evoke maximum delight, maximum satisfaction for her as a woman. Yet when he looked into her eyes she could see he wasn't blasé; this meant something to him, too. At his core was a vulnerability that bonded her to him in a way that mere physical pleasure could never accomplish.

Nicola's orgasm was followed quickly by Aidan's release so that they seemed to soar together. Afterward, even though the sex was over Aidan was still looking at her as though she was the most beautiful woman in the world. Then it struck her that at this moment, to him, she was. The revelation brought a smile to her lips.

Tracing the upward curve of her mouth, he said, "You look like the cat that ate the canary."

She wrinkled her nose. "*Eew.* Don't like feathers."

"No regrets?" he asked, searching her face.

"Just beautiful memories." Her smile faded at the thought that their time together would be so short. This closeness, this sense of rightness couldn't be wrong or fleeting. Why hadn't she asked for more than the holiday period? Her feelings wouldn't fade once Christmas passed.

With his finger he gently pushed at first one corner of her mouth then the other. "Let's see that cute grin of yours."

She slid a hand over his chest, relishing the feel of his smooth hard muscles. "Make love to me again and I'm sure I could find something to smile about."

Much later, exhausted and satiated, Nicola snuggled into Aidan's side and closed her eyes. Just for a few minutes, she thought, then she'd go back to her own bed....

"Noooo!" Nicola cried, her splayed hands thrust before her.

In suffocating blackness she lurched upright in bed, heart pounding, eyes straining to adjust to absolute dark.

She'd pushed Charmaine over the cliff.

It was only a nightmare, she assured herself as she slowly regained her presence of mind. But imprinted on her brain was the mental image of her cousin's terrified face as she fell to her death.

Aidan rose on his elbow and touched her cheek. "Are you all right?"

"I'm fine," she managed to say. "I had a bad dream."

He gathered her in his arms and pulled her close, pressing kisses on her temple. "Want to tell me about it?"

She shuddered. "No."

Nicola lay back on the pillow, comforted by Aidan's presence and the weight of his arm curled around her. Before long his even breathing indicated he'd lapsed back into sleep. She was tired, too, but guilt and doubt were keeping her awake.

She turned her head to watch Aidan sleep. The tiny line that normally furrowed the gap between his eyebrows had smoothed away, leaving his face younger-looking and peaceful.

Aidan had given her a precious gift; he'd made her feel like a beautiful and desirable woman.

He'd also loved Charmaine with all his heart. *Still* loved her. He'd said it himself, *Charmaine is a barrier to me committing to another woman.*

Nicola had loved Charmaine, too, but sometimes she hated her cousin. Were Aidan's feelings as mixed up as hers?

She suddenly remembered Charmaine's letter. It was still in the pocket of her cargo pants, packed away in a plastic bag in June's spare room cupboard along with the rest of her old clothes. She'd been so busy the past two days she hadn't had time to read it or even remember to bring it with her.

Never mind, she would get it tomorrow.

WHEN AIDAN AWOKE the next morning Nicola was gone. For a moment he wondered if he'd imagined last night until he put his face to her pillow and breathed in her scent. He ought to be grateful she'd gone back to her own room before Emily had woken, but his body was hardening with the memory of their lovemaking and he wished she'd stayed just a little longer.

There was a knock at the door and Nicola came in carrying a steaming cup. Her hair was wet and slicked back and she was dressed in her bathrobe, a bulky terry towel affair that looked two sizes too large. "Would you like some coffee?"

"Thanks." He took the cup and set it on the bedside table before drawing her down beside him. Smiling into her eyes, he took her mouth in a long leisurely kiss. "Come back to bed."

"Can't," she said regretfully, sliding away. "Emily's up. She'll be bounding in here any minute. Drink your coffee but don't take too long. I'm making pancakes."

Over breakfast Aidan suggested a trip to Whistler so Emily could see Santa Claus.

Emily's eyes grew round. "Can we go right now?"

"Finish your pancakes first," Aidan admonished.

"Could we stop by June and Roy's first?" Nicola asked. "I forgot…some clothes I wanted to bring."

"No problem," Aidan replied.

But when they got to Emerald Estate, June and

Roy's cars were both gone, the house was locked up tightly and there was no response to the doorbell.

"I don't have a house key," Nicola said, dismayed. "I used the one attached to June's car key ring."

"We'll come by again later," Aidan promised.

Whistler Village square was a winter fairyland with colored lights strung through trees and decorations in all the stores. Shoppers strolled through the snowy streets laden with parcels and a man was selling roasted chestnuts. In the distance the faint jingling of bells sounded in the crisp clear air from the horse-drawn sleigh rides. On a temporary platform in the middle of the square a large chair covered in red velvet was set up for Santa to receive his young visitors.

"She's nearly too old for this." Aidan felt a bittersweet pang as he and Nicola watched Emily perch on Santa's knee. "They grow up so fast. I wish—"

Nicola glanced up at him, her cheeks rosy. "You'd had more children?"

He nodded, hesitated, then asked, "Do you want kids?"

"More than anything," she said wistfully. Then as if realizing she'd made herself vulnerable, she added briskly, "When I find the right man, that is. I'm in no hurry."

"You want to get it right the first time, that's for sure," Aidan replied, thinking of Charmaine.

Emily came running back to them, a candy cane clutched in her mittened hand. "Can we go home now, Daddy?"

"Sure, kiddo." He put a hand on her shoulder and guided her through the throng toward the parking lot.

"What did you ask Santa for?" Nicola asked Emily when they'd left the crowds behind.

Aidan held his breath. Now that he and Nicola had become lovers Emily's wish list might be a tad embarrassing.

"Stuff," Emily said, busily unwrapping her candy cane, adding with a sly smile, "Daddy knows."

Nicola grinned. "Looks like you'd better come through with the goods, Dad."

If she only knew what she was saying. Aidan gave a lopsided smile. "Emily knows even fathers can't perform miracles."

"At Christmas they can," Emily said confidently and stuck her candy cane in her mouth.

He ruffled her daughter's hair affectionately. "You've been watching too much TV. I have a day off tomorrow. What do you say the three of us go skiing?"

Emily's eyes widened in disbelief. Nicola grinned. "Do you mean it?"

Their delight convinced him he'd made the right decision. "Absolutely. It's time I taught my daughter how to ski."

THE NEXT MORNING Nicola again jumped out of Aidan's Land Cruiser with a promise that she'd just be a moment and knocked on her aunt's door. "Hello!" she called as she turned the handle and pushed the door open. "It's me, Nicola."

June appeared in the hall outside the kitchen. "We're just having breakfast. Come and join us."

"Thanks, but I can't," Nicola said, going to meet her. "We're going skiing. Aidan and Emily are waiting for me in the car. Hi, Grammy. Did you sleep well?"

Her grandmother smiled at her from the table. "Lovely, thank you. I appreciate your giving up your room for me." She paused. "Is everything going all right at Aidan's?"

Nicola smiled, blushing a little. "Couldn't be better."

"Good," Grammy said with satisfaction. "Although I hope I'm going to see something of you while I'm here."

"I'll come over during the day when Emily's at school." Nicola turned to June. "I came to pick up some clothes I left in the cupboard in the spare room."

"Go ahead," June replied. "If you want to borrow Charmaine's skis they're in the garage."

"They might be a bit long for me but I'll try them.

It'll save me having to rent some." Nicola excused herself and ran upstairs to the spare bedroom.

Grammy had hung up her clothes in the closet. Nicola pushed aside some long skirts and the black coat to get at the plastic bag with her cargo pants. Then she stared in disbelief. The carpeted floor inside the closet was bare except for three pairs of Grammy's shoes. Her bag of clothes were gone!

"Aunt June?" she called as she hurried back down the stairs. "Have you moved my bag of clothes from the cupboard? There was a pair of cargo pants I particularly wanted."

Frowning, June sipped her coffee. "Roy took our discards to Goodwill yesterday. Don't tell me your things got mixed up with ours."

"They must have." Nicola fought down a sense of panic. "Where is the Goodwill store?"

"Pemberton," she said, mentioning the small town thirty minutes drive north of Whistler. "I'm so sorry. Are the pants that important?" She paused and added delicately. "I'd love to take you shopping for some new things. It could be my Christmas present to you."

She'd already bought new clothes but June didn't know that because Nicola had gone to stay at Aidan's the same day.

"Thanks, but I really need *those* pants. You see,

I—" Nicola broke off. If she told June about Charmaine's letter and then didn't get it back June would feel so much worse than if she never knew about it. "I have a sentimental attachment to them," she finished lamely.

"Why don't you call Goodwill and see if they've sold the pants yet?" Grammy said practically. "If not, you can buy them back."

"I know the woman who runs the store. I'm sure she'll hold them for you." June was already looking up the number in the local phone book. "Here we are…" She picked up the phone and dialed then gave the handset to Nicola. "Good luck."

"Hello?" Nicola said when a woman answered the phone. "My uncle brought in some bags of clothing yesterday and a pair of my cargo pants were included by mistake. Do you by any chance still have them? Dark brown. Sure, I'll wait." She held her hand over the mouthpiece and said to June and Grammy. "They're checking."

A few minutes or so later the woman came back on the line. "Oh, no!" Nicola said when told the pants had already been sold. "Do you know who bought them?"

June's eyebrows arched. To her mother she murmured, "She must really love those pants!"

Nicola hung up and faced her aunt and grandmother unhappily. "She doesn't know. The girl who was working yesterday isn't in again until tomorrow."

Outside, a car horn beeped.

"Aidan!" Nicola cried. "I've got to run. I'll see you soon."

She went out through the garage, collecting the skis on her way. Aidan got out and strapped them onto the roof with his. "What took you so long?"

"Roy took my clothes to the Goodwill. I was trying to track them down. Without success." Frowning, she worried her bottom lip between her teeth and added to herself, "There's still a chance I'll find them."

Nicola forced herself to put the cargo pants and their hidden letter out of her mind. Once they were on the mountain, it wasn't hard. She spent the first hour helping Aidan teach Emily the rudiments of skiing but when he suggested she take the opportunity to ski by herself she agreed readily. Looking after Emily hadn't allowed her much time for what had once been her favorite sport.

After arranging to meet them at the Roundhouse Lodge for lunch she rode the chairlift up to Little Whistler Peak. The steady whine of the lift was muffled by her thick padded hat and the sky above was bright but overcast with solid white cloud cover.

Below, ski huts buried up to their eaves in snow looked like Arctic hobbit houses.

She chose an intermediate trail and started her descent, taking it easy at first, gradually building her confidence. Considering she'd been away from the sport for years she thought she was doing pretty good. Exhilarated from her successful run she got straight back on the chairlift and returned to the top.

She set off once more and this time when she spied a black diamond marker she branched off onto the advanced trail. Her cockiness was short-lived. The perfect weather had attracted lots of skiers to the slopes. Too many. When she made a clumsy turn and inadvertently cut someone off she realized her skills were too rusty to cope with the more difficult run.

She headed to the right-hand side of the slope where there were fewer skiers. With no sun to cast shadows that would aid depth perception, the hill appeared to be a smooth, even mantle of snow. This proved to be an illusion. The run was riddled with moguls that were impossible to see until she was flying over them. Her legs ached with the effort of controlling her descent.

She was nearing the end of the run, and not a moment too soon, when the tip of her right ski caught as she landed on the far side of a mogul. Down she went, in a tangle of skis and limbs, wincing as her knee twisted when the boots didn't come away from the bindings as they were supposed to. She fell heavily, knocking the wind out of her. For a moment all she could do was lie there cursing Charmaine's old skis and herself for not checking them over more thoroughly.

As she was struggling to release her bindings so she could straighten her leg, a ski patroller in a gray-and-white jacket swooped upon her and came to a halt in a spray of snow. He removed her ski, giving her instant relief from the pressure on her knee and helped her to a sitting position with her leg stretched out before her.

"Are you okay?" he asked, peering into her face with bright blue eyes. Wisps of blond hair emerged from the brim of his knitted hat. As he spoke he ran his hands down her leg, checking for fractures.

"I'm fine." She started to move and yelped in pain, rubbing her knee.

He gently probed the joint. "You've probably strained the ligaments. Nothing a little ice and elevation won't fix. My name's Rich. I'll take you down the mountain to the clinic."

"Oh, but I'm supposed to meet Aidan at the Roundhouse. Aidan Wilde. He's a patroller, too. Can't I just go to him?"

Rich hesitated, considering the matter. "Regulations say I have to take you right down the mountain, but if you're with Aidan I know you'll be in good hands. First I've got to get you that far."

He got on his two-way radio and put in a call to Dispatch. "Christy, I've got a 10-7 on Camel Back. I need a Code 1. Over."

While they waited, Rich said, "Aidan and I have worked together for years. In fact, we used to be partners."

"Really?" Nicola said. "What a coincidence."

"I'm surprised he's up here on his day off," Rich said. "He usually spends all his spare time with his daughter."

"He's teaching Emily to ski. They're down on the bunny hill at Olympic Station."

Another patroller appeared, pulling a rescue toboggan.

"I'm not that badly injured," Nicola said, trying to stand.

"You don't want to make it worse," Rich said, putting a hand on her shoulder to stop her from rising. "I'll splint that knee and give you a ride down to bump."

He worked quickly to bind her knee with first-aid supplies brought with the toboggan, then assisted her into the sled. Nicola felt a bit silly about being towed along like a child but had to admit she would have found skiing or even walking down the mountain unaided next to impossible.

A few minutes later she was sitting on a wooden bench with her leg up on a chair and an ice pack on her knee. A pair of off-duty patrollers sat at a table on the far side of the room, playing cards. In the dispatch office next door, a pretty young woman with a long blond ponytail whom Nicola assumed was Christy was stationed in front of a computer while a two-way radio crackled and jabbered in the background.

Rich handed Nicola a cup of coffee and some anti-inflammatory tablets. "You probably shouldn't ski anymore today. But I know Aidan will make sure of that."

Nicola glanced at her watch. "I'm supposed to meet him and Emily at noon. It's already eleven-thirty."

"Plenty of time," Rich assured her. I'll take you to him, but first I'm going to rewrap your knee." He knelt in front of her and removed the temporary splint. Glancing up at her with a friendly smile, he asked, "Are you the woman Aidan's taking to the Christmas Ball?"

She felt herself blush. "How did you know?"

"Patrollers are a tight-knit bunch." He bent over

her knee and began to expertly wind on a tensor bandage. His pink scalp showed through his thinning blond hair. "You're Charmaine's cousin, aren't you?"

"Yes. Did you know her?" Nicola asked.

"I used to go out with Charmaine before Aidan. She was pretty special."

Nicola waited a moment before saying quietly, "You must have been upset when she died."

Rich's hands stilled. "Very much."

"Were you on the mountain that day?"

He rocked back on his heels to gaze up at her, his face serious. "You should talk to Aidan about this."

"He's told me some things but it's very painful for him." Hoping she wasn't somehow betraying Aidan, Nicola took a deep breath. "Please tell me what you know. Charmaine wasn't just my cousin, she was my best friend."

Rich silently finished bandaging her knee. Nicola had the feeling he was debating her request. Finally he attached the clip to hold the end of the bandage in place.

"She came up on the chairlift just before it was closed due to hazardous conditions," he said. "She asked me where Aidan was. I knew, but I tried to convince her to go back down to base. She wouldn't hear of it."

Nicola gripped the foam cup in her hands so hard

it bent. Another witness. Why hadn't Aidan mentioned Rich? "Why was she there?"

Rich started to gather up the splint and the ice pack.

"Please?" Nicola said, fearing he was going to leave without saying anything more. "It's really important to me."

"She didn't tell me that." He frowned, his mouth twisting, as if he were concentrating hard, trying after all these years to figure out what had been going on in Charmaine's head. "She seemed desperate," he said at last. "As if she had some hugely important task that she had to perform at all costs."

"But there was a blizzard," Nicola protested. "How could you let her go out on the mountain?"

His gaze shot to hers. "Short of wrestling her to the ground there was no stopping her. I knew Aidan was working on the far side of the permanently closed area so I told her where he was, then followed at a distance after radioing ahead to warn him she was coming. Charmaine foolishly took a shortcut across the closed area, instead of going around. I called out to warn her, but she ignored me. Then Aidan saw her and went to meet her."

"So you were watching them." Nicola's eyes widened. "What happened?"

Rich's gaze turned distant, focused on the past. He

spoke softly, with a kind of abstract horror. "I saw her take a bundle out of the front of her jacket. Aidan shouted something at her and she set it down on the snow. That's when Aidan yelled to me to go get help. I didn't see Charmaine go over the cliff." Rich paused, his face pale. "It might have been better for Aidan if he'd had a witness."

Nicola could hardly take in what he was saying; it was more than Aidan had ever told her. "A bundle? Do you know what it was?"

"I couldn't *see* it very well, but…" Rich looked her straight in the eyes. "It's impossible to mistake a baby's cry."

Nicola's ears started buzzing and the room seemed to spin. *Charmaine had taken Emily up the mountain.*

She felt a strong hand gripping her shoulder, another taking her coffee cup. "Are you all right?" Rich asked. "Didn't Aidan tell you this?"

Dazed, Nicola shook her head. "Why would she take a two-month-old baby up the mountain in a blizzard? It's even more incomprehensible than her going herself."

"I and another patroller came back with a rescue sled to find Aidan in a state of shock," Rick went on. "Charmaine had fallen off the cliff. The other patroller radioed for an ambulance. I told Aidan he should go to base but instead he took Emily down the mountain and gave her to Charmaine's mother."

"June was there, too!" Nicola's eyes widened. Certain things her aunt had said made sense now. Sort of. Nicola felt weirdly disoriented. In spite of their antipathy, Aidan and June had colluded in some sort of cover-up regarding Charmaine's death.

"I shouldn't have told you." Rich berated himself. "Aidan swore me to secrecy. But I figured you being Charmaine's cousin, it wouldn't matter if you knew." He shrugged helplessly. "And after all these years, I needed to tell someone."

He looked so miserable Nicola put a hand on his shoulder. "Secrets can be a burden. Aidan would know better than anyone."

She looked at her watch again and tugged down her pant leg. "I'd better go."

Rich helped her up and handed over her gloves and hat. "Are you sure you're okay?"

"I'm fine," she lied. She wasn't fine at all. Her knee was throbbing and her heart ached with the new revelations about Charmaine. After the intimacy she and Aidan had shared, how could he have failed to tell her this crucial piece of information?

Rich took her arm and she leaned on him as he escorted her to the front of the Roundhouse Lodge. Waiting at the foot of the massive stone steps were

Aidan and Emily. Emily nudged her father and pointed. Nicola waved as she limped forward.

"What happened?" Aidan demanded, coming to meet them. "Nicola, are you all right?"

"Yes, thanks to Rich." She smiled at the other patroller.

"I found her on Camel Back with a twisted knee," Rich said. "I iced the joint and bandaged it. She should be fine in a day or two."

"Thanks." Aidan took Nicola's arm. "Let's go."

"Bye, Rich," Nicola said. "Thanks again."

"You're more than welcome. See you at the Christmas Ball." Rich lifted his arm in farewell. "Save me a dance. Oh, Aidan," he added, delaying their departure. "My interview is tomorrow morning. Has yours been scheduled?"

"Tomorrow afternoon." Aidan paused before adding a terse, "Good luck."

Nicola glanced awkwardly from him to Rich, aware of the tension between the two men. Competing for a job both wanted couldn't be easy, but she sensed their rivalry went deeper, right back to Charmaine. Everything, always, came back to Charmaine.

CHAPTER TWELVE

THE DRIVE HOME was full of tense silences. Aidan seemed lost in dark thoughts of his own and Nicola couldn't get Rich's words out of her mind. Charmaine had taken Emily up the mountain that fateful Christmas Eve. Why? And why hadn't Aidan told her?

At the red light he turned to her. "You're very quiet. Does your knee hurt?"

Her *feelings* hurt. Aidan's tender, passionate lovemaking and his unabashed pleasure in her friendship with Emily had given her hope. A hope that despite what he'd said about Charmaine being a barrier to commitment he might come to care for her longterm. Now she found out he'd been keeping a huge secret from her all along.

"Nicola, your knee, is it okay?"

She roused herself to look at him. She prayed that when they had a chance to be alone again he would tell her everything, without reservation. She didn't care if he'd done something wrong, as long as he was straight with her.

"It's throbbing a little. The tablets Rich gave me took the edge off the pain."

Aidan paused. "Is anything else bothering you?"

Nicola glanced over the back seat at Emily who was drawing faces in the condensation on the window and talking to herself as she played some private game. She was occupied but that didn't mean she wasn't listening. "It can wait."

The light changed and Aidan put the car into gear and moved forward. "Marc and Fiona are back from Greece and everyone is meeting at Mom and Dad's tonight. Emily is counting on showing you off to her aunts and uncles. Will you be able to come?"

What she really wanted to do was talk, but that wouldn't be an option anyway if he was going out. "I'll put another ice pack on my knee as soon as we get home. I should be well enough by tonight to go to your parents'."

In Tapley's Estate all the houses were lavishly decorated, turning the entire subdivision into a celebration of Christmas. Emily raced up the steps of Leone and Jim's house and rang the doorbell of the log home strung with merrily blinking colored lights.

Nicola barely had time to admire the homemade wreath of pinecones and holly when the door was opened by a woman with softly wavy auburn hair, wearing a dress of dark green wool.

"Here you are! Come in." Leone Wilde stepped back to allow them entry. "We were wondering if you would make it in this snow. Have you ever seen such a winter? Emily, how are you, dear?"

"I went skiing!" Emily bounced up and down. "And I can roar like a lion. Roar!"

Leone laughed, a hand pressed to her chest and looked at Aidan in amazement. "Who *is* this child?"

"It's me, Emily!" the girl shouted.

"So it is." Leone stooped to give her a big hug.

"Nicola," Aidan said. "You remember my mother, Leone."

"How are you, Leone?" Nicola said, extending her hand.

Leone ignored her hand and pulled her into a warm embrace. "It's lovely to see you again after so long. You look marvelous."

"Thank you." Nicola was glad she'd chosen to wear one of her new outfits, an ivory blouse over black silk pants. Aidan's eyebrows had risen when she'd come out of her room and his admiring smile had made her feel sexy and feminine.

Leone led the way past a vaulted living room with Haida masks hung above the high stone hearth toward the back of the house and the sounds of laughter and glasses clinking.

"We used to have more contact with Charmaine's family, but since the accident, well…" Leone trailed off, noticing Nicola's limp. "Did you hurt your leg?"

"I fell on the ski slope today. It's nothing."

They reached the family room and a dozen pairs of eyes turned to them. Nicola instinctively shrank back but Aidan grasped her by the hand, drawing her into the midst of the group. "Come and meet everyone. You know Angela and Nate, of course. Do you remember my father, Jim?"

Nicola waved to Angela and Nate and shook hands with the tall, dark-haired man with silver at his temples. She could see where Aidan and Nate got their good looks. "Nice to see you again."

Aidan continued with the introductions. "This is Angela's sister, Janice, and her husband, Bob," he said, indicating a less glamorous version of Angela and a lanky brown-haired man. "Kerry and Tony," he went on, nodding at an attractive chestnut-haired woman and her blond companion. "Frederik, my partner, and his girlfriend, Liz." The tall, shaved-headed man had his arm around a woman with short dark curls.

Nicola murmured greetings and tried to remember everyone's name. Her attention was drawn to a woman with lively features and a mass of red-gold curls, who was standing beside a ruggedly handsome man with dark blond hair. The man, who looked vaguely familiar, sat in a cushioned wicker chair with a walking stick propped at his side. The woman's hand rested on his shoulder. Both looked tanned and relaxed.

"You must be Fiona and Marc," Nicola said, feeling comfortable enough to release Aidan's hand and introduce herself. "How was Greece?"

"Fabulous," Fiona said, extending her hand with a smile. "But it's good to be home."

Nicola turned to Marc, remembering why his face looked familiar; before the bomb blast that injured his back he'd been a well-known TV journalist reporting the news from the Middle East. "It's nice to meet you."

Marc braced one hand on the arm of the chair and the other on his walking stick and rose. With a slight stiffness in his gait, he moved the few steps to shake her hand. "Anyone who can get Aidan to attend the Christmas Ball has to be pretty amazing."

"Doesn't he go every year?" Nicola asked.

"Not since before Emily was born. He hardly goes out at all anymore." Marc leaned on his walking stick to throw an affectionate punch at his cousin. "Not for want of encouragement from his family."

"Aidan took Emily skiing," Leone informed them with a meaningful look at Nicola. "I think someone has influence."

"Look out, Nicola," Angela said, grinning. "Aidan must have really fallen for you."

"Cut it out, guys," Aidan growled. "You're making her uncomfortable."

It was true that Nicola felt her cheeks grow warm at their good-natured teasing but inside she was bursting with pride. Of all the women in Whistler, he'd chosen her to take to the Christmas Ball. He *must* have real feelings for her. It was almost enough to make her forget the secret he'd kept from her. Maybe, she reflected, feeling charitable, he had a good reason for that.

"Don't listen to them, Nic." Aidan pulled her into the kitchen and put a steaming glass filled with spiced red wine into her hand.

She glanced up, startled at his use of her childhood nickname. "You called me Nic."

"Charmaine always called you that when she spoke of you, which was often," he said. "You don't mind if I call you Nic, too, do you?"

She smiled at him. "All my close friends do."

He touched her chin, bringing her head up, and studied her face. "That would include me, I hope."

Leone approached with a plate of savories, her

gaze flicking from one to the other. "Curry puff? They're a family favorite."

"Thanks," Nicola said, accepting a fragrant triangle of puff pastry.

"Aidan, would you pass these around for me?" Leone asked, handing him the plate.

"Excuse me a minute," Aidan said to Nicola. She nodded and watched him move back to the group.

"I'm pleased you got Aidan to take Emily up the mountain," Leone said to Nicola.

"What makes you think it was me?" Nicola asked.

"It has to be you with all the changes happening in my son's life lately," Leone replied. "Emily's really come out of her shell. She was always such a quiet little mouse and now she's literally roaring."

"I *am* responsible for that, I'm afraid," Nicola admitted shamefacedly. "I never thought she'd take to it so enthusiastically."

"There's nothing to be apologetic about." Leone glanced at Aidan across the room in a tight circle with Nate and Marc, his head thrown back, laughing. "Whatever you're doing, keep it up. Aidan seems happier than I've seen him in a long time."

"I'm glad," Nicola said and sipped her wine.

"He needs to settle down again." Leone put her arm around Nicola and squeezed. "We're all hoping you'll stay around for a good long time." Her eyebrows rose, questioningly.

There was no mistaking her meaning; she was sounding Nicola out about her intentions toward Aidan. "I'm going away on a photography assignment in January, but I have to admit, Whistler still feels like home." She paused then added wistfully, "I'm not sure Aidan's completely over Charmaine."

A cloud crossed Leone face. "Something's been eating at him all these years. I don't know what, unless he feels guilty over not being able to save Charmaine. He had counseling after the accident and he has family to confide in but he still has this unnatural reserve. One thing I do know, he may be the most private of my boys but he isn't a loner by nature."

So even Aidan's mother wasn't privy to the whole story. That made Nicola feel a little better until she reflected that whatever Aidan was hiding must be pretty bad if he hadn't told his family. It also appeared powerful enough to have kept him single all these years.

The timer on the stove dinged. Taking up a pair of oven mitts from the counter, Leone removed a tray of stuffed mushrooms from the oven and transferred them to a plate. She offered one to Nicola then excused herself to take them around the room.

Nicola stayed on the sidelines, gaining pleasure

just watching the warmth and closeness so evident among Aidan's family.

Aidan returned to put an empty plate on the counter. "Are you taking mental notes about the Wilde family quirks?"

She smiled wryly; he wasn't far from the truth. One thing she'd noticed was that Angela was the only one not drinking mulled wine. "Among other things, I was thinking how much you seem to enjoy each other's company."

"We are lucky, I know." He moved beside her to gaze out at the others. "I can't believe the change in Marc. At one time his doctor told him he'd never walk unaided. When he and Fiona left on their honeymoon he could barely stand and only take a few steps. Now he's walking almost normally."

"He's made a remarkable recovery," Nicola agreed. "It just goes to show how the body can heal." She hesitated then looked at him before adding, "Hearts, too."

Aidan's gaze flicked away. "Marc just told me his father, my uncle Roland, is flying in Christmas Eve. They've been estranged since Marc was a teenager but after Marc's accident they patched things up."

"I'm happy for him." Nicola sighed. "I wish my parents could be here."

"I know you've got your aunt and uncle," Aidan

said, "but I think after tonight you can also consider yourself an honorary Wilde. Everyone's taken to you…you can tell by the teasing."

"I guess I'd better get used to it then." She smiled. "Leone made me feel really welcome."

Again he glanced sideways; this time his gaze lingered. "Did you and Mom have a nice conversation?"

"Is that a roundabout way of asking what we talked about?" What could she say—*Leone seems to want me as a daughter-in-law?* She could hardly believe it, as much as she wanted to. "I like your mom a lot." She paused. "She thinks you still feel guilty over Charmaine's death."

"Guilt is a wasted emotion," he said as if reciting facts learned by rote. "Charmaine's death was an accident. I have to accept that under the circumstances I couldn't have saved her."

"That sounds all very rational, but do you believe that in your heart?"

A telltale crack appeared in his composure, just a tightening of the skin around his eyes and mouth, but it was enough to convince her he didn't.

Before either of them could say anything else Nate started tapping his glass with a spoon. "Attention, everyone! Ange and I have an announcement."

"Nate!" Angela rolled her eyes, blushing furiously. "Why not shout it from the front doorstep?"

Wrapping an arm around her waist, he grinned down at her. "I just might do that."

By this time a hush had fallen over the room. Leone edged her way to the front of the circle of family and friends. "Is it good news?"

"We're expecting," Angela blurted.

"The baby's due in July," Nate added, looking every inch the proud father-to-be.

Everyone crowded around the happy couple, engaging in much hugging, back-slapping and heartfelt congratulations. The pregnancy was especially welcome since Angela had miscarried ten years ago, early in their marriage. And the July due date was deemed highly appropriate as that was when Nate and Angela had renewed their wedding vows. Nicola offered her good wishes and wondered wistfully if she would be around to see the newest addition to the Wilde family when he or she came along.

As she and Aidan drove home later that night she studied his profile, silvered by the moon, shadowed like a sculpture. The past and Charmaine loomed over them like a cloaked intruder, overshadowing the temporary high brought on by the evening with his family. Nicola was torn between causing Aidan pain and her need to unravel the mystery about Charmaine. He'd all but admitted to feeling guilty over her death. What role had he played in the tragedy?

Emily was already in her pajamas, fast asleep in the back of the car and safely strapped into her seat belt with a blanket tucked around her.

"Rich told me Charmaine brought Emily up the mountain the day she died," Nicola said quietly.

Aidan cursed under his breath. "He promised he'd never tell."

"I dragged it out of him. Why are you so afraid of people knowing?"

"It's a long story."

"I've got all night."

He took his hand off the steering wheel and dragged it through his hair. "Okay, but first let me get Emily to bed. I can' take a chance on her waking up and hearing what I have to say."

Nicola had been tired but now she was keyed up. At last she would learn what really happened to her cousin. She had a feeling she wasn't going to like the truth. The biggest question in her mind was, would knowing make her feel differently about Aidan?

Aidan parked in the carport and carried his sleeping daughter into the house. Nicola shut and locked the doors behind him then made a pot of decaf coffee. Aidan was stoking up the fire when she carried in the tray.

Nicola handed him a cup and sat on the love seat. "Well?"

Aidan went to his recliner and contemplated what he was about to reveal. He, June and Rich—an unlikely alliance if there ever was one—had kept their dark secret too long. This was the moment he'd dreaded for years, yet now that it was here he approached it with an almost fatalistic relief.

Nicola deserved to know the truth and Aidan wanted to tell her. He risked losing her but he couldn't lie to her another minute, either by omission, or in fact.

Even though he knew Emily was in bed sound asleep, he glanced over his shoulder just to be absolutely certain she wasn't around. Then in a low voice, he said to Nicola, "There are things I've told no one, not even the police."

She leaned forward. "What are they?"

There was no other way to say it but straight out. Even so, his voice dropped to a hoarse whisper as if by speaking quietly he could lessen the impact of his words. "Charmain tried to kill Emily."

Nicola's mouth dropped open, her eyes wide with shock and disbelief. "Oh, my God. She wouldn't have harmed her own baby, surely."

"I wouldn't have believed it myself if I hadn't been there, but it's true. You didn't see her in her depressed state. She wasn't herself—she never smiled or laughed, she was completely withdrawn. It was like living with a stranger." He paused, unable to go on as memories washed over him at seeing her so ill and feeling powerless to help. "I think it was the idea of our baby having to endure multiple operations and endless testing and after all that maybe not even surviving that tipped her over the edge. I worried that Charmaine might inadvertently harm Emily through neglect but I never considered for a moment she might do so deliberately. I should never have left her alone, not for a minute."

"You shouldn't blame yourself," Nicola murmured.

"But I do." Remorse and self-reproach, his constant companions for the past six years drew his mouth into a tight downward curve. "I never should have left her alone, not for a minute. I tried to arrange my schedule so that someone was always with her—I didn't seriously think Charmaine would deliberately harm Emily, but that she might inadvertently do so through neglect. That Christmas Eve it just wasn't possible."

"What happened?"

"I was called in to work on an emergency. A skier was lost and they were already one patroller short due to someone going home sick. June and your grandmother were doing last-minute Christmas shopping in Vancouver. My mother was working."

"Couldn't you have called one of her friends to stay with her?" Nicola asked.

"We'd turned into hermits by this time," Aidan said. "Charmaine refused all contact with friends. I tried anyway, but couldn't get hold of anyone on such short notice. In the end I went to work, having contacted June on her cell phone and asked her to come to the house as soon as she could. Charmaine insisted she'd be fine." He swallowed. "Believing her was the biggest mistake I ever made."

Tucking her legs up, Nicola wrapped her arms around her knees and rocked. "Do you really think Charmaine took Emily up the mountain planning to…" She trailed off, as if unable to speak the words.

Aidan nodded, his eyes shutting briefly in pain. "When I came up to her she took Emily out of her baby carrier. She had this wild look in her eyes. She…she said, 'I'm going to kill this baby.'"

Nicola gazed at him, horrified. "I can't even begin to imagine what must have been going through her head. How was she—?"

"By throwing her over the cliff, or leaving her in the snow…who knows?" Aidan dragged a hand down his face. "It wasn't her fault," Aidan immediately defended her. "She was ill. She didn't know what she was doing. You have to believe that."

"I do. Of course I do," Nicola assured him. "I

knew Charmaine. She had her weaknesses but in her right mind she would never have hurt anyone, let alone her own baby."

"Emily was blue with cold," Aidan went on, his hands tightening around his coffee cup. "I thought… I was afraid she was already gone. But when I picked her up she was still breathing. She started to cry. I noticed Rich a ways off. I called to him, told him to get help. Then I started to put Emily inside my down jacket. I told Charmaine I would never allow any harm come to our baby—" He broke off.

"Go on," Nicola whispered.

"Those were the last words I said to her. The top layer of snow where Charmaine was standing sheared off. She started to slide backward, as you almost did that day we went up the mountain. I might have caught her, but—" He broke off, swallowing convulsively. "I had Emily half in, half out, of my jacket. I was afraid of dropping her. It took only a second to secure her but by the time I reached for Charmaine…" He choked. "It was too late."

"Oh, Aidan." Nicola slid off the couch to go to him, hugging him hard. Tears slid down her cheeks.

Aidan buried his face in his hands as guilt swamped him. "It's my fault she's dead. It's my fault my baby almost died."

"You had a split second to choose between rescuing your baby or your wife," Nicola said. "No wonder you feel guilty—but you're not to blame."

Still with her arms around him, she frowned. "I don't understand why there was nothing of this in the newspapers. How could the police not know Emily was there?"

"She barely made a bump inside my thick jacket. After I reported the accident I tried calling June again. She'd just dropped your grandmother off at home and was on her way to be with Charmaine. She came to the mountain instead and took Emily back to her house."

To keep her safe. "Why didn't you tell the police afterward?" Nicola persisted. "Surely it was relevant."

Aidan lifted his shoulders in a helpless shrug. "Charmaine was dead and no harm had come to Emily. What was the point in making Charmaine look like an unfit mother and fueling gossip in the Valley for the next fifty years? I couldn't bring Charmaine back but I could protect her reputation and Emily's image of her mother."

"So you copped the gossip in Charmaine's place," Nicola concluded. "Weren't you afraid Emily would grow up wondering if you killed her mother?"

"It never occurred to me at the time that anyone would think that," he admitted. "Even if I'd been able to foresee the future I would have done the same. It was all I could do for her by then."

"Poor Charmaine," Nicola said. "I wish I'd been there for her."

"I wish *I'd* been more vigilant. I should have stayed home that day or made sure someone was with her. whether she wanted company or not."

"You said it yourself—you can't predict the future. You couldn't know what she was going to do, Aidan. You didn't kill her."

His eyes squeezed shut. "I might as well have. I feel as though I did."

"Emily's lucky you found her in time, before—"

Aidan reached for Nicola's hand and gripped hard. "You're not to breathe a word of this to my daughter or anyone else," he said fiercely. "I will not have her knowing her own mother tried to kill her. Even though Charmaine wasn't in her right mind and couldn't be held responsible it's too horrible. Emily believes her mother loved her more than anything else in the world. I want her to always believe that."

"I swear to you I would never let Emily think anything else."

Nicola fell silent, swamped with emotion, hardly able to get her mind around all she'd been told. The fire crackled and hissed, accompanied by the quiet ticking of the mantel clock.

Aidan was staring into the fire, his face a mask of pain. He was punishing himself with guilt, had been for years. Suddenly she no longer wanted to find Charmaine's letter. Recalling a phrase she'd read... *want to end Emily's misery...* Nicola realized with a sickening lurch of her stomach just how devastating those words would be to Aidan. She would do anything to spare him further misery.

She loved him. It wasn't infatuation, or chemistry, or a longing for the attentions of an attractive man. Nor was it the immature desire to outdo Charmaine. Nicola wanted to absorb his pain and give back happiness, to be his comfort and joy, his haven from remorse, a bright star guiding his path.

She might not be able to do all that, but she would do what she could, starting with showing him her feelings toward him hadn't changed. Rising, she took his hand.

His gaze met hers, questioning.

Softly she said, "Let's go to bed."

CHAPTER THIRTEEN

AIDAN THOUGHT they wouldn't make love, but when Nicola came into his arms, his desire for her was even stronger than before. They made sweet slow love that was healing and bittersweet, and somehow deeper and more intimate because now Nicola knew the truth.

Afterward, she lay with her head on his chest and he wrapped his arms around her. She stirred now and then to ask for more details on this point or that. Eventually she drifted off and Aidan lay awake, thinking how lucky he was. He'd told her everything and she hadn't run away.

Well, almost everything.

He awoke at his usual time hours before dawn. Wintry moonlight was seeping through the cracks in the curtains. Nicola was staring at the ceiling, her expression thoughtful.

He slid an arm around her under the covers and snugged her in close. "What are you thinking?"

"I was thinking about something Rich said. He told me Charmaine asked for you when she got off the chairlift. Why would she do that if she was planning to harm Emily?"

"I had no idea she asked for me. Rich never said." Taken aback at this information, Aidan flopped back on the pillow. "Why would she?" he mused. "Unless she wanted to stay away from where I was." Then he shook his head. "It doesn't really change anything, not given what she said to me."

"I guess." Nicola was quiet again for some minutes.

"Anything else on your mind?" he asked. "Might as well clear everything up at once."

She propped herself on one elbow to face him. "Were the newspaper reports right? Did you and Charmaine have marriage problems?"

Here it was, his final confession. "Everyone thought we had the perfect relationship, when in fact—"

"You don't have to go into detail," Nicola said. "I think you've answered my question."

"No, I want to explain." Shifting to a more comfortable position, with his head propped on his pillow against the backboard, he said, "Charmaine was like a very beautiful, very charming, Mack truck—overwhelming everyone in her path. Part of me will always love her but it wasn't until a few years into our marriage that I realized how great the differences between us were."

"I always thought you two were well matched," Nicola said. "Now that I know you better I must admit you're not the party animal I assumed you were."

"Children tend to change your priorities. When Charmaine and I first got together I was into downhill racing, and the pub scene and the parties that went with it. That was fun for a while, but even before Emily came along I was getting tired of it. Charmaine craved bright lights, people, lots of attention."

Nicola nodded. "She was an outrageous flirt."

"At times she went beyond flirtation…but I won't go into that." Even now, humiliation and resentment surfaced at memories better left unmentioned. "I grew tired of her constant demands. She was unhappy, because I didn't want to spend three or four nights a week at the pub and I refused to pander to her every whim." He paused and caught Nicola's sympathetic gaze. "Charmaine never wrote to you about this?"

"She always pretended you two had the perfect marriage." Nicola was quiet a moment then began to speak, plucking at the sheet with her fingernail. "I've been jealous of her all my life. She was so beautiful and charming and everyone loved her instantly. I had to work hard to make friends and as for guys, forget it." Nicola grimaced shame-facedly. "I sound petty, don't I? In spite of everything I've just said, I did love her. But I loved her in spite of her faults, not because she didn't have any."

"So did I, as far as I could. She just wasn't the right woman for me." He breathed a quiet sigh and tilted Nicola's chin so she was looking at him. "I can't tell you what a relief it is to talk to someone who understands."

"I know what you mean. I don't dare say anything even slightly critical about Charmaine around June and Roy. Not that I would anyway. I accepted Charmaine for who she was a long time ago."

Aidan smoothed a strand of hair behind Nicola's ear. "Too bad you can't accept yourself that easily."

Nicola made a face—half smile, half grimace. "I'm working on it."

"I'd fallen out of love with her by the time she died," Aidan went on. "I keep wondering if I could have saved her if I'd loved her more."

Nicola shook her head. "I don't believe that for a minute. But why did you stay with her if you no longer loved her?"

"Charmaine resisted any talk of divorce, not wanting to be the one who was dumped. I told her she could tell everyone *she'd* left *me,* but that wasn't good enough. Then she got pregnant. She put pressure on me to stay and I agreed to try again."

"Do you think she deliberately got pregnant to keep you?" Nicola asked.

Aidan shrugged. "Who knows? Whether Emily's conception was an accident or an attempt at manipulation, she's the best thing that ever happened to me. I will never regret that we had her."

The radio alarm clicked on. He drew Nicola close for a lingering kiss then reluctantly let her go. "I've got to go to work. In a few days I'll be off until after Christmas and we'll have more time together."

"That'll be nice." Nicola wriggled deeper into the covers. "See you this afternoon."

Aidan rose and reached for his jeans where he'd dropped them on a chair the night before. "I'll be home late. My interview is at five o'clock."

"Good luck," she said. "Not that you need it."

He drew on his shirt and blew her a kiss before going out and shutting the door. Nicola listened to him quietly moving around the kitchen and savored the homey domestic sounds of him getting his breakfast. She heard the fireplace door open and knew he was stoking the fire so that when she got up in another hour the house would be warm. Feeling cosseted and cared for, she reset the alarm and shut her eyes for a little more sleep.

NICOLA WAS MAKING Emily's after-school toasted cheese sandwich when the phone rang. "Hello? Oh, hi, Aunt June."

"Hi, Nicola. Marjorie from the Goodwill in Pemberton called," June said. "She talked to her assistant and got the name and address of the girl who bought your pants."

Nicola paced the floor space between the counter and the stove. "That's amazing."

"Not really. All the locals know each other around here. Anyway, the girl hasn't worn them and is happy to return them for a refund. I'll pick them up for you this afternoon after I go to the Pemberton florist for decorations for the Christmas Ball. You haven't forgotten it's this Friday, have you?"

"No, but don't bother with the cargo pants. I've decided I don't...." She broke off. On second thought, she didn't want this girl to read Charmaine's letter. If everybody knew each other here she might easily figure out who Charmaine was and what the letter was about. Even if Nicola had no stomach for reading about Charmaine's last hours the letter needed to be in safe hands.

"Thanks, Aunt June," Nicola said, instead. "I appreciate you doing this."

"Do you want me to drop them off at Aidan's house?"

"No, thank you. I bought a few new clothes when I was in Vancouver. Could you put my cargo pants back in the closet? I'll be by to get them soon."

Over the next few days Nicola visited with Grammy and helped June with some of the preparations for the ball. After school she played with Emily, sometimes taking her to Leone's to bake Christmas cookies. But she never did look for the cargo pants in the guest-room closet. Charmaine's letter, once a discovery to be treasured, was now a nightmare to be avoided.

THE EVENING of the Christmas Ball, Terri, the teenage girl from down the road who baby-sat occasionally, fed Emily dinner while Aidan and Nicola disappeared to their rooms to get ready.

A half hour later Aidan was pacing the living room, glancing at his watch. What could be keeping Nicola? She wasn't the primping type. All she had to do was throw on her dress and comb her hair. He had champagne on ice and good news he wanted to share with her.

His high spirits dimmed momentarily as he recalled Rich's too-enthusiastic congratulations that afternoon, followed by the "accidental" spilling of coffee over the official letter informing Aidan of his promotion. It was a childish stunt unworthy of Rich, but it left Aidan in no doubt how badly Rich had wanted the job and how much he resented Aidan for besting him.

Emily and Terri were bent over the coffee table, engrossed in putting together a jigsaw puzzle of Santa's workshop that Terri had brought. Terri, her black hair falling around her face in long layers, was still turning over pieces while Emily, who couldn't wait to get started, was trying to fit together two pieces that didn't go.

"Don't force them," Terri said. "Why don't you start by gathering all the edges you can find?"

"Did you feed the fish today, Emily?" Aidan asked, stopping in front of the tank. Tiny blue neon tetras darted among the waving grasses, while two fat black-and-white angelfish swam slowly through the surface layers.

"Yes, Daddy. Do these go together, Terri?"

Their voices faded into the background as Aidan gazed at the fish and thought about his pact with Nicola. He was supposed to forget the past and she wouldn't think about the future. Nothing wrong with that as far as it went. The problem was, lately he couldn't stop thinking about the future and how lonely it would be without her. Surely there was no harm in sounding her out about her plans after her photography assignment was over. Depending on her reply he might suggest she return to Whistler for a while, see how they felt about each other.

Emily gave a sudden squeal of excitement. Aidan straightened away from the tank.

Nicola was dressed for the ball. Not in the dowdy black dress but in the shimmering silver-blue creation. She'd put her hair up, revealing an elegant neck and shoulders, and put on just enough makeup to enhance her delicate features. He opened his mouth to say something but couldn't speak. Words seemed inadequate to describe Nicola's transformation from plain Jane to the luminous beauty that stood before him.

Terri's mouth was hanging open. "You look awesome."

Emily stood and jumped up and down on the love seat, her cheeks flushed. "You got the pretty dress!"

"Don't jump on the couch, Emily," Aidan said absently, unable to take his gaze off Nicola.

"Do you like it?" Nicola asked him.

"You look sensational. When did you go back to the store?"

"The day I picked up my grandmother from the airport." She smiled into his eyes. "I decided it was time I came out of hiding."

Aidan went to the sideboard and poured the champagne. Handing her a flute of bubbly, he said, "That alone is worth celebrating. To your metamorphosis."

She raised her glass and clinked with his. "Cheers," she said and drank. "Is there more to celebrate?"

"The head of Human Resources called me in to her office today." He couldn't contain his grin any longer. "I got the job."

"Oh, Aidan, that's wonderful." Nicola set her glass on the table and threw her arms around his neck. "Congratulations!"

Aidan hugged her, breathing in her faint perfume, and felt his heart swell and his body tighten. Yes, tonight was a night for making plans and dreaming big dreams. Go slowly, he cautioned himself, don't scare her by coming on too strong.

Drawing back, he toasted again. "To the future and my new job."

Nicola winked. "And to the marvelous present."

"Christmas present?" Emily interjected excitedly. "Where?"

Aidan and Nicola laughed.

NICOLA WALKED into the Christmas Ball on Aidan's arm feeling like a princess. Heads turned as they went past and men's gazes lingered. On *her*. One young man gave her a wolf whistle, making her blush and giving her a heady sense of feminine power. She pinched herself. Any minute she'd wake up and the fairy tale would be over.

A twenty-foot Christmas tree dominated one end of the ballroom, twinkling with colored lights and sparkling with decorations. Crimson candles surrounded by pinecones and holly adorned each linen-draped table and on the far side of the dance floor a long buffet groaned with roast turkey, baked ham and silver chafing dishes of hot vegetables along with salads and rolls. On the stage opposite the tree, a band was setting up. Hundreds of women and men dressed in evening gowns and tuxedos milled through the ballroom, champagne glasses in hand, their combined voices raising the noise level to a roar.

Nicola waved to her aunt and uncle across the room and plucked a champagne flute off the tray of a passing waiter. "I think I'm actually going to enjoy this."

Aidan gave her an amused glance. "I'd hate to think your aunt and her friends went to all that effort to give people a lousy time." He craned his neck to look across the room. "Nate and Angela snagged a table. Shall we join them?"

Nicola nodded and they waded through the crowd

with frequent stops to chat with Aidan's friends and acquaintances, all of whom wanted to be introduced to Nicola.

"If I remember a tenth of their names I'll be lucky," she murmured as they moved on after one such encounter. "Do you know *everyone* in Whistler?"

"I'm not sure about that," he demurred, "but it would appear that everyone I know is gathered here tonight."

Marc and Fiona had arrived and were sitting at the table when Nicola and Aidan got there. Angela removed her evening purse and shawl from the chairs she'd saved for them.

Nicola greeted the other couples then glanced at the remaining two vacant chairs next to her. "Should we be saving those for Leone and Jim?"

Nate shook his head. "They're sitting with friends. Keep an eye out for Kerry and Tony, though."

"I saw Kerry in the ladies' room," Angela said. "They're sitting with some of Tony's filmmaking friends who came up from Vancouver for the weekend."

Tables were filling fast and there were few empty places left when a woman asked Nicola, "Are these seats taken?"

Nicola smiled, recognizing the pretty blonde from the Dispatch office. "Please, be our guest."

The woman waved across the tables to someone in the crowd around the bar. "Rich! Over here."

Nicola turned to Aidan in delight. "Rich and his date are joining our table." She was surprised to see his good-humored expression grow somber. "What's the matter?" she asked in a low voice. "Isn't that all right?"

"Rich didn't take the news that I got the assistant manager's position very well."

"Oh, dear. This could be awkward."

"It's fine," Aidan muttered. "Don't worry." He leaned forward and introduced Nicola to Christy.

Rich strode over, a drink in each hand, and his smile faded slightly when he saw Aidan. Nicola began to wonder if she'd made a huge mistake inviting Christy and Rich to join them, but what else could she have done?

"Evening, everyone." Rich put on a hearty smile and pulled out the last empty chair. "Aidan, I see you got out of your mercy date—" He broke off, belatedly recognizing Nicola. "Nicola! Have you, er, done something different to your hair?"

Nicola forced a laugh. "Among other things."

Mercy date? She glanced at Aidan expecting him to refute it, but he was too busy glowering at Rich.

Rich covered his gaffe by giving her an admiring glance. "Whatever you've done, it's working. You look fantastic. If Aidan's ever busy, give me a call."

Before she could figure out how to reply to that, Aidan spoke up. "She's not going to be in Whistler long."

Nicola's fledgling confidence wavered. Aidan still saw their relationship as temporary? Had she only imagined they were closer now than before he'd told her about Charmaine? Could he have tired of her even and didn't know how to tell her?

Then she became impatient with herself. How could one stupid comment throw her into a tizzy of insecurity?

"Too bad," Rich said. "Aidan, I'm glad to see you you're not too grand to consort with the peons now that you're management." Although Rich was smiling there was a distinct edge to his voice.

Aidan returned his smile, but he, too, sounded strained. "You know lording it over the troops isn't my style, Rich."

The band, a twelve-piece ensemble, began to play a swing tune. Aidan touched Nicola's shoulder. "Let's dance."

Nicola followed him onto the floor. Aidan proved to be an excellent dancer; she supposed life with Charmaine had given him a lot of practice. When a slow dance started he drew her into his arms and rested his chin next to her temple.

Nicola couldn't keep silent long. "What did Rich mean by 'mercy date'?"

Aidan's grip on her tensed. "I don't know what he was talking about. Pay no attention."

Nicola didn't find his manner entirely convincing. Pulling away so she could see his face, she said, "Did you ask me tonight just be kind?"

He drew her back against him before he answered. "I asked you because I wanted to."

Nicola thought about this. His family seemed to think she was the reason he'd attended the ball at all. But in spite of how well she'd "scrubbed up" tonight, hitherto she'd been pretty drab. Sure, she and Aidan got along well but after Charmaine could he really be *attracted* to her?

"Because it wasn't necessary," she couldn't help saying. "I would have been happy to stay home."

"Can't you just accept that I asked you because I like you?" Aidan said, sounding a little exasperated.

Like, not *love.* Maybe it was too soon to be talking about love although she was certain that's what she felt for him. "Would you have asked someone else if I hadn't been in town?"

"Please, just drop it."

But she found she couldn't. Like a worm in an

apple, doubt was eating its way to the heart of her. If this was a "mercy date", did that make their love-making "mercy sex"? She thought back to the night they'd first gone to bed together. Aidan had said he found her desirable. Wouldn't *any* man who hadn't had sex in a while find *any* seminaked woman he came across desirable?

She hated second-guessing everything Aidan had said and done. Where had her confidence gone? Aidan was here with her. Wasn't that good enough?

Rich suddenly appeared beside them, winking at Nicola and tapping Aidan on the shoulder. "May I cut in?"

"No," Aidan replied.

Rich gave Nicola a sad dog face, pretending to be desolate. *"Awww."*

"Of course you can," Nicola said, overriding Aidan. Her ego badly needed a boost.

She almost changed her mind when she saw the black look on Aidan's face and the bitter triumph in Rich's eyes. Too late she realized Rich wanted to get the better of Aidan and she was his means to an end. They rhumbaed and tangoed their way through the next two songs and when another slow song played Rich pulled her into his arms.

"Won't Christy be wondering where you are?" Nicola said uncomfortably.

"She won't mind. She's probably cozying up to Aidan right now."

What was he trying to insinuate? Nicola glanced over her shoulder, trying to catch a glimpse of their table. Sure enough, Christy and Aidan had eliminated the empty chairs between them to sit side by side, chatting. Nicola had been hoping he'd come back and dance with her.

"What did you mean earlier when you asked Aidan if he'd gotten out of his mercy date?" she asked Rich.

A tinge of red rose in Rich's cheeks. "I, uh, I was just joking."

"No, you weren't."

"Okay, if you really want to know, Christy asked him to go with her and he didn't want to. He needed an excuse fast so he used you. He told her his late wife's cousin was in town and didn't know anyone so he had to take her."

Nicola felt as though she'd been slapped in the face. "He did not say that."

Rich shrugged. "I was standing right there."

"When was this?" Please let it be after he'd already asked her. Maybe he'd phrased it that way to let Christy down easily.

"Let's see…" Rich thought a moment. "It was the day we learned that Bob was retiring early and his job was coming vacant."

The day she'd moved into Aidan's house to look after Emily. Aidan hadn't asked her to the ball until the evening of that day, after he came home from work. Her heart started to hurt. Christy was pretty and seemed very nice. "Why would Aidan turn her down?"

Rich shrugged. "He's got this rather arrogant notion that a certain kind of woman can handle a fling and another kind can't. He won't go out with anyone he can't drop without feeling guilty. I've heard him talk about it before. He probably believed Christy would have made demands he couldn't fulfill."

And Nicola wouldn't. She'd told him she was all for living in the present. He wouldn't even have to drop her because she wouldn't be in town long enough for a serious relationship.

Nicola felt her face grow hot just thinking about it. She sensed Rich watching her. He had a smirk on his face that wasn't nice, but his words had the ring of truth. Now that she thought about it, Aidan's invitation to the ball *had* seemed to come out of the blue.

Aidan was gun-shy when it came to relationships. Fool that she was, she'd gone and fallen for a good-looking guy way out of her league. Had he made love to her because he felt sorry for her? Oh, that would be the worst.

The song ended and the lights came up, signaling

the band was taking a break. Nicola smiled and started to draw away. "Thank you for the dance."

Rich tightened his grip on her. "Aidan doesn't deserve a hot-looking babe like you," he said and kissed her.

Nicola was so startled she didn't pull back at once. But when his kiss became insistent and she felt his tongue pressing unpleasantly at her closed lips she pushed hard on his chest. He stepped back, eyes glittering.

She turned to leave and came face-to-face with Aidan.

"That's enough, Rich," Aidan said, advancing on the other man. "I'm not going to stand by this time."

"Lighten up, Wilde, it was just a kiss. Catch you later, Nicola." Rich tipped his finger to his forehead in a cocky salute before he strode off.

"Are you okay?" Aidan asked, reaching for her.

"Fine," she muttered, sidestepping his hand. She started walking toward their table.

"What's wrong?" Aidan demanded, catching up with her in two strides. "What did Rich say?"

Nicola stopped to face him in the middle of the deserted dance floor. "Did you invite me to the Christmas Ball to avoid going with Christy?"

Aidan's grimaced and clenched his hands into fists. "Are we back to this again?"

"We're back to this because you didn't tell me the truth the first time."

"I didn't tell you a lie."

"A lie by omission is still a lie," she said hotly. "Rich told me he was standing right there when Christy asked you and you told her you had to take Charmaine's cousin. Do you have any idea how sick I am of getting a date because of Charmaine?" Nicola threw her hands up. "She's dead and it's still happening. I can't believe it."

"Right now, Rich will say anything to make me look bad," Aidan said. "I *wanted* to take you."

"But that's not why you asked me in the first place, is it?" she demanded, searching his face for mitigating factors. *Say you saw the real me beneath the bulky clothes and the nondescript hair, that you love me for who I am, that you chose me over all the beautiful women.*

Aidan pushed a hand through his hair, messing it up. He looked extremely frustrated. "No, but…that was then."

He hadn't asked her because he wanted to go with her; he'd simply wanted to get out of a sticky situation with another woman.

"You wanted me to be honest," he said, exasperated.

Suddenly she realized they were alone on the dance floor, having an argument. Curious gazes drifted their way. Mortified, she wanted to run and hide, to fade into the background like the wallflower she really was. Instead she was highly visible in a glitzy dress that screamed *look at me*.

She ran back to the table and gathered up her evening bag, avoiding the anxious eyes and worried questions directed at her by Angela and Nate, Marc and Fiona.

Aidan followed her all the way to the exit, demanding in an undertone that she stop and talk to him. Head high, she kept on walking. If she stopped moving, she'd start crying. She had enough pride left that she didn't want to break down in front of all these people.

At the door she ran into June and Roy and was brought to an abrupt halt, struggling to maintain her composure.

"Nicola!" her aunt exclaimed. "Your dress is fabulous. Are you having a good time? Everyone's saying this year's ball is the best yet."

"That's wonderful, Aunt June." Nicola forced a smile. She glanced at Aidan who paced nearby, throwing tense glances her way. "I'm moving back to your place if that's all right. Aidan is off work till after Christmas so he doesn't…need me…anymore." She choked out the last few words.

June glanced from Nicola to Aidan, belatedly realizing something was amiss. "Of course. We'll make up the bed in the loft."

"Don't worry. I'll sleep on the couch in the family room."

"You're perfectly welcome to stay at my house," Aidan interjected, coming closer. To June he added, "I know you've got your mother staying, too."

Nicola sent her aunt a pleading look.

"We'll do whatever Nicola wants," June said firmly. She hesitated, her worried gaze fixed on Nicola's face then said bravely, "You can use Charmaine's room."

"Are you sure?" Nicola said.

Biting her lip, June nodded.

Roy put an arm around his wife. "I'm proud of you."

"Thank you," Nicola said to them both, afraid she might burst into tears out of gratitude if not heartbreak. "I...I don't feel well. I'm going to take a taxi home."

June reached into her purse and withdrew a set of keys which she gave to Nicola.

"I'll drive you," Aidan said.

Roy stopped him with a hand on his arm. "Let her go."

"Nicola!" Aidan called.

She glanced back, tears filling her eyes. "Whatever we had—it's over."

Nicola threw her wool wrap around her shoulders and got her coat from the cloakroom and ran down the steps to where a line of taxis waited. As she jumped into the lead cab she glanced at her watch. It was a couple of minutes to midnight.

She told the driver the address, then sank back into the seat. Both her high-heel shoes were still on and her feet were firmly on the ground. Prince Charming would not be coming after this bogus princess.

CHAPTER FOURTEEN

NICOLA LET HERSELF into June and Roy's darkened house and tiptoed upstairs. Soft snores coming from the guest room told her Grammy was fast asleep. The door was ajar so Nicola quietly pushed it open and snuck inside to retrieve her bag of clothes from the closet. It was nearly full; June must have got most of her clothes back. Somewhere in there was an old flannelette nightgown.

Nicola backed out, and went down the hall to Charmaine's room. She took off her dress and hung it in the closet. Aidan was right—she would never wear it again. She sat on Charmaine's bed in her nightgown and clutched her cousin's teddy bear to her breast. She would not cry over Aidan. She absolutely would not. Her five minutes of happiness had all been a glorious, fleeting dream.

She'd fallen in love with a man who'd only pretended to like her. Oh, he probably *liked* her well enough, but he didn't *love* her.

She would leave tomorrow to wherever she was supposed to meet Reiner—Banff or Aspen, she couldn't remember. She had plenty of photographs of Whistler; Reiner could come here later to do his own research. She would go away and never come back. She would forget all about Aidan. It would be easy.

Nicola sat on the bed and dug back into the bag for the cargo pants. She slipped her hand into the right pocket and felt the crinkle of airmail paper. A mixture of relief and dread flooded through her. Still holding Charmaine's teddy bear she unfolded the letter with trembling hands.

> *Dear Nic,*
> *It's the afternoon of Christmas Eve and it's snowing a blizzard. Emily is finally sleeping. I'm sorry I haven't written for so long. I haven't been myself lately. Poor Emily's been impossible today, crying and crying. I wish I could end her misery.*

Nicola felt a deep shiver spread from her shoulders down through her arms and into her legs. Knowing what she knew now, she wanted to tear the letter into tiny pieces. Aidan would find it incredibly painful and as betrayed as she felt, she didn't want to inflict any more grief on him. Showing the letter to her aunt seemed equally out of the question. June would probably insist it was a forgery. Roy would get impatient with his wife's refusal to face facts and have another Scotch, which would, in turn, create even more distance between them.

But Nicola knew she could no longer hide the truth, no matter how horrible. She made herself read on.

> *I'm sorry I haven't written for so long. To tell you the truth I'm a mess, so depressed I can hardly get out of bed in the morning. I didn't write to you after Emily was born because, well, she has serious problems with her spine. How can I tell you how it feels to carry a baby for nine months then to give birth and discover your child has a possibly life-threatening congenital abnormality? Mom won't even talk about it. Aidan is trying to help but he doesn't really understand. The antidepressants take time to work, they say, but right now I feel as though there's no point in living.*
>
> *Damn it. Emily's crying again. In other times, in other societies, she wouldn't have been allowed to live.*

Nicola put down the letter, feeling sick to her stomach. For Charmaine to even contemplate hurting her own baby was like a nightmare. It was as if she were possessed by some evil alter ego. Even her writing had taken on a different character, becoming dark and jagged. Nicola didn't want to read any more but she had to.

She won't stop crying. I'm so afraid of these wild, angry feelings clamoring inside me. I watch the fish tank hoping the gentle movements of the angel fish will bring me peace. Sometimes it works. Not today. I'm going out of my mind. I tried to change Emily's diaper and ended up shaking her. I can't go on, Nic. I've made up my mind, I'm taking Emily up the mountain.

Charmaine's scrawl had become almost illegible toward the bottom of the page. Nicola, her heart pounding even though the words had been written six years ago, turned the page, anxious to read what happened next and at the same time dreading confirmation of her worst fears.

I'm taking her to Aidan. Mom isn't home and neither is Leone. I can't call anyone else. I wouldn't want them to see me like this. Aidan is the only one I can trust to care for Emily, to protect her from me, her own mother, and not

*to say anything. He'll be angry that I've taken
her out in a blizzard but I don't care. I can't be
trusted with my own baby anymore. All those
things I said about her not being perfect? I
didn't mean it. She's the most beautiful baby
in the world. I love her so much even if sometimes I can't feel it. I'll finish this when I get
back but I have to go now before I do something really horrible to her—*

There the letter stopped.

Tears streamed from Nicola's eyes. The letter
dropped out of her hands and fluttered to the floor.

Charmaine hadn't taken her baby up the mountain
to kill her. She'd tried to save her.

All these years, the truth had been hidden away
in a box of abandoned Christmas decorations. All
these years, Aidan's heart had been locked up in a
torment of grief and guilt.

All these wasted years.

There was no question now that she had to show
him the letter. But the agony of going over there, seeing him so soon after their fight. How would she explain to Emily why she left so abruptly?

Oh, what did it matter what she would say or how
she would feel? For Aidan to know the truth was
more important.

AIDAN HEARD THE DOORBELL and stuck a last strip of tape on the Christmas gift he was wrapping for Nicola. She probably didn't want anything from him after the way they'd parted but he hoped he could still give it to her.

Who could be here so early the morning after the Christmas Ball? He'd left shortly after Nicola, but he knew most people would have partied on until the small hours.

Nicola stood on his doorstep, snowflakes dotting her hair and shoulders. Dark circles rimmed her eyes as if she'd had a sleepless night. Damn Rich for opening his mouth and hurting her feelings. No, that wasn't fair. He, and he alone, had hurt Nicola.

"Come in." He stood back to let her enter.

"Who is it, Daddy?" Emily came running from her room. "Nicola!" The girl flung her arms around Nicola's waist. "Have you come back to stay with us?"

Nicola hugged Emily and met Aidan's gaze over the child's head. "No, honey. I came to talk to your dad."

Aidan's eyebrows rose. Was this her final goodbye? "Go finish tidying your room, Em. When Nicola and I are done talking she'll come and see you." He glanced at Nicola for confirmation and she nodded.

"Okay," Emily said reluctantly and left.

"Do you want some coffee?" Aidan said, leading

the way into the living room. "Some of Mom's mince tarts?"

"Nothing, thanks." Carrying her backpack Nicola perched on one end of the love seat.

Aidan sat opposite her on his recliner, wondering what this was all about. It hardly seemed possible he'd been laughing with and making love to this woman just a few days ago. And yet she didn't seem hostile, just…drained. "I'm sorry about last night—" he began

She stopped him with an upraised hand. "That's not what I came about."

"What is it then?"

"The night we decorated the tree I found a letter from Charmaine in the box, addressed to me," Nicola said in her usual direct manner. "It was dated December 24, the day she died."

Aidan's heart seemed to stand still. For a moment his brain was frozen, too. Then he stirred as the implications sunk in. "Why didn't you tell me about it then?"

"I didn't have a chance to read it before you came into the room so I shoved it into my pocket for later. I wanted to know what she'd said before I showed you in case…" She trailed away.

She didn't need to elaborate. Emily had been

there. Nicola hadn't brought it out in case Charmaine's words were too awful for Emily to hear.

"What about afterward?" he asked.

"I left the letter in the pocket of some old pants which were being stored at June's house. I went for it once but no one was home. Then Uncle Roy took the bag of my clothes to the Goodwill by mistake."

"But you somehow got it back and have now read it," he guessed, aware his heart was beating faster than normal.

She nodded, tears seeping into her eyes.

"Well?" he demanded. "What did it say?"

Nicola undid the top flap of her back pack, removed two folded sheets of blue airmail paper and handed them to him. "Read it for yourself."

With shaky hands he unfolded the flimsy paper and held it in the light of the table lamp. *Dear Nic, It's the afternoon of Christmas Eve…* His eyesight blurred as memories of that day rushed forth in a jumble of terror and grief. Blinking he forced himself to read on.

An involuntary groan was wrenched from his throat when he came to the part where Charmaine spoke of not wanting to go on living.

"I didn't fully understand the seriousness of her condition or I never would have left her alone," he said. "Not for anything."

"You had no other option," Nicola reminded him.

"If you'd stayed, the person lost on the mountain might have died. You did what you thought was right."

Aidan said nothing; it had been a day of tough choices. He went back to the letter. As he read Charmaine's comment about how Emily wouldn't have been allowed to live in some societies, anger overwhelmed his guilt, making him forget momentarily that she couldn't be held accountable for her actions, or even her words. "What right did she have to make life and death decisions about our baby?"

"Read on," Nicola urged. "Just read."

He turned over the page. There were only a few lines left but they told a story so different from what he expected that he had to scan them twice before he took in the meaning.

At last Aidan lifted his astonished gaze to Nicola. "She was bringing Emily to me for safekeeping."

Her cheeks wet with tears, Nicola nodded. "She loved Emily and didn't trust herself."

"Oh, Lord. All these years I was telling Emily the truth about her mother and didn't even know it." His breath caught in a racking half sob, half laugh, and he had to clutch himself to keep in control. Then, suddenly, he lost his grip on his emotions and tears flowed down his cheeks.

"It's all right." Nicola crossed the space between them to sit on the arm of his chair and put her arms around him. "You're going to be okay. Don't try to hold back your feelings. Let them go."

"Oh, Charmaine, I'm so sorry. S-so s-sorry." Had he ever really cried for her before? There'd been a tear or two of hot anguish squeezed between clenched eyelids, but not like this. Not these huge, body-shaking, cleansing sobs. Throughout, Nicola clung to him, holding him together, making sure he didn't fly apart.

Gradually he became conscious of a vast relief welling up through the layers of sorrow and pain. On this flimsy piece of paper the real story was written. Charmaine had died, not trying to kill their baby, but trying to save her. Never again would he worry that his daughter could be hurt by the knowledge that her mother had tried to harm her.

Emily was safe.

He wiped his eyes with the back of his hand, more at peace than he'd been in years. "I feel as though I've been released from prison," he said to Nicola. "You've given me my wife back. You've given me my *life* back."

Nicola gently disengaged herself from his embrace. "I'm so glad. What will you tell Emily?"

He smiled. "I don't have to tell her anything. She already knows the essential truth—her mother loved her and Charmaine's death was an accident."

Aidan sobered as he became aware that the ache

hadn't completely dissolved, that a splinter of remorse was permanently lodged in his heart. "I'll always feel a certain responsibility for the tragedy," he
said, "but at least now healing is possible."

He glanced up at Nicola. "Have you told June
and Roy?"

Nicola shook her head. "I wanted to show you the
letter first."

"If you don't mind, I'd like to tell June myself."

"Of course."

Aidan thought for a moment and added, "I'd also
like to take Emily up Whistler Mountain for a small
ceremony on Christmas Eve to commemorate Charmaine's death. And her life." He reached for Nicola's hand. "I'd like it very much if you came."

"I don't know," she said uncertainly. "It sounds
like a private thing for you and Emily."

"I was going to ask June and Roy, too."

"I can't." Nicola withdrew her hand. "I'm leaving
today."

His heart lurched. "Before Christmas?"

She shrugged as if she couldn't trust herself to
speak and got up to pace across the room. "I want to
get a head start on photographing Aspen. June and
Roy don't have room for me with Grammy here,
anyway. I've had a good visit."

Aidan couldn't bear to think he'd driven her away.
"I wish you wouldn't go."

She bit her lip and blinked a few times.

"Daddy?" Emily appeared in the hallway, her child's sixth sense telling her something was up.

Aidan was torn between trying to get Nicola to stay longer and wanting to reconnect with his daughter. Even though he'd said nothing had changed, in his heart he felt a strong desire to reinforce to Emily that she was loved and wanted, not only by him but by her mother before she died. "I'm coming, honey."

"I have to go now," Nicola said and rose.

She went to Emily and crouched to give her a hug. "Take care of your daddy." Then she leaned closer and whispered something in Emily's ear that made the girl smile.

"I'll walk you out." Aidan waited while she put on her boots and coat and hoisted her backpack over her shoulder. Was it his imagination or did it appear lighter than when she'd come in?

Outside on the steps, he said, "I never meant to hurt you, Nic."

Her eyes pressed shut. "I know."

His plan to ask her to return to Whistler after her photography assignment seemed a lifetime ago, a notion formed by another man. But he couldn't bear to let her walk away from him; the loss hurt more than he could have guessed.

"I'm sorry Rich told you how I came to invite you to the Christmas Ball," he said, "but I'm even sorrier I didn't tell you myself. Can we try again?"

She gave him a trembling smile, her eyes full of pain. "I've always been a realist. I don't blame you for what happened but I've decided I won't ever let myself feel second best again. Now that you're free of the past you need some time to figure out who you really want in your life."

Aidan couldn't speak a word in response to that. His mind was confused, chaos reigned in his heart and his emotions were ragged and raw. What he came up with seemed inadequate. "I hope we'll always be friends."

"I'm sure we will." Nicola's quiet smile was tinged with irony. "I've had a lot of experience being buddies with attractive men."

He winced at that. "You deserve someone special."

"Don't worry about me," Nicola said. "It's better I know the score now than wait until I do something stupid like—" She broke off to swallow, holding his gaze with a sad sweet smile.

Like fall in love with him?

"What?" he said.

She shook her head. "Nothing."

Before she could move away he leaned over and kissed her. It was a bittersweet farewell, salty with the taste of tears and already heavy with nostalgia. "Thanks for all you've done for Emily."

"I loved being with her." Her voice sounded thick, as if tears had piled up in her throat. And then she was hurrying down the steps to her car.

He was still standing on the porch, freezing in his shirtsleeves when Emily came and led him by the hand to the Christmas tree. Nicola had left two gaily wrapped presents beneath it, one for him and one for Emily. He hadn't had a chance to give her anything.

AIDAN CRAMMED the next few days with activity to fill the gap left by Nicola's departure. He took Emily skiing again, attended a goodbye party for Bob and his wife who were taking off on an extended holiday to the southern United States and he bought a new couch to replace Charmaine's antique settee.

"It's so comfortable, Daddy," Emily said, lying full-length on the plum-colored microsuede. "I wish Nicola could see it. When will she come back?"

Aidan picked up his daughter's feet so he could sit. "I don't know, Em, she didn't say. But probably not for a long time."

"At least I've got a picture of her," Emily said.

"You do?" Aidan's gaze shot to her. "Let me see it."

Emily ran to her bedroom and returned with a slightly off-kilter photo of Nicola at the kitchen counter, making a cheese sandwich. "I took it myself on her camera."

Aidan took one look at Nicola's smiling face and his heart turned over. Honesty, warmth and humor shone in her eyes, character and strength were evident in the stubborn tilt of her chin.

And if he loved her, why had it taken him so long to recognize it? And what was he going to do about it?

NICOLA GAZED OUT the window of her hotel room in Aspen at the falling snow and wondered for the millionth time what Aidan and Emily were doing. It was December 23 and in the days she'd been here she'd taken enough photos to fill ten coffee-table books. Not only that, she'd turned into a regular shopaholic, buying a complete replacement wardrobe and even got a stylish new haircut.

June and Roy had been unhappy and bewildered when she'd left so abruptly—and Grammy, who guessed the real reason, had been positively angry.

"Running away from love," she'd said to Nicola, shaking her white head. "I thought you were all grown up, but you're behaving like a schoolgirl."

"Aidan doesn't love me," Nicola had told her, stuffing sweaters and jeans into her suitcase.

"How do you know what he feels?" Grammy said. "*He* doesn't even know."

"Oh, he knows all right," Nicola replied, sitting on her suitcase to get it to close. "He wants us to be friends."

"That doesn't mean he doesn't want more," Grammy said stubbornly. "If you'd only give him time."

Nicola picked up her suitcase and cameras and headed for the stairs.

"You'll be a wallflower all your life if you leave now," Grammy warned, following her down the stairs.

Nicola paused to study herself in the hall mirror. Her scoop-necked sweater was more feminine than she was used to though not as daring as what Charmaine used to wear. Which was fine, she thought; *this is me*.

"No, I won't." She flicked her straight brown hair out of her eyes. "Now that I've decided to look my best I owe it to myself try out other men besides Aidan."

"Don't change too much," Grammy scolded Nicola. "Remember who you are inside. Don't be too proud to come back if you want to. And don't give up on Aidan."

In Aspen Nicola flirted with a ski instructor, had

dinner with a public relations employee and danced the evening away with a guest from the lodge. She realized it wasn't so much looks but confidence that men found attractive. But although all her dates were appealing in their own way, none engaged her emotions the way Aidan had.

Nicola sighed, remembering her Grammy's parting words. She'd been so scared of her feelings for Aidan that she'd run away without thinking. There was nothing shameful about falling in love. Who knows, maybe Grammy was right and Aidan just needed time to sort out his feelings.

She wished now she'd stayed for the ceremony for Charmaine; she would have liked to say goodbye to her cousin. She would have liked another conversation with June once her aunt knew the truth. She would have liked to see Emily open her Christmas presents. She would have liked to make love with Aidan one more time....

Oh, what was the use in pretending? She had no reason to stay in Aspen and a whole lot of reasons to go back to Whistler. Goodness knows, she had her own weaknesses and faults but pride had never been one of them.

The phone rang but she made no move to answer it. She didn't want to make excuses why she couldn't go dancing as she'd tentatively promised last night's dinner companion. Instead she got up and packed her bag. The ringing continued for a good few minutes. Jim, or Tim, or whatever his name was, was certainly persistent. Just as well she was leaving.

IN THE PREDAWN SKY on Whistler Peak the last star winked in the pearl-gray morning of Christmas Eve. A light breeze brought an extra chill but it chased the clouds away, leaving the air crystal clear.

Aidan held Emily's mittened hand in his, looking over the snowy peaks to the east. Under his other arm he carried the heavy urn containing Charmaine's ashes. To his right June and Roy waited silently, deep in thoughts of their own, no doubt about their daughter.

He'd ferried them up on the snowmobile before the lifts opened for the day, first June and Emily, then Roy. June and Roy as much as he, didn't want curious onlookers to witness their private ceremony.

He found himself thinking, not of Charmaine, but of Nicola, and wishing she was with him. He'd missed her—badly. The niche she'd carved in his heart with her laughter and her funny stories had become an aching hollow now that she was gone. The pain grew with every passing day.

He considered her parting suggestion that once he was free of the past, he would find out who he wanted. Well, that person was her. He'd called her last night to tell her so, only to hear the phone ringing and ringing. She hadn't checked out of the hotel so she must have been out. With someone else? A sharp stab of jealousy made his brows crease in a frown.

"The sun is coming up." Roy's voice interrupted his dark musings.

Aidan shook his head, clearing it. Sure enough, pink and orange streaked the sky over the mountains. "Let's get started."

The muffled roar of an approaching snowmobile broke the stillness. Aidan turned toward it, irritated when he saw Rich in the driver's seat. He waited while the machine came to a halt and a passenger dismounted. Female by the look of the slim curves beneath the raspberry-colored ski suit. For an instant he entertained a wild hope she was Nicola but the stylish short haircut squashed that idea.

Rich waved once then roared off. The woman started toward them. Aidan blinked, hardly believing his eyes. He knew that tomboyish stride.

Emily recognized her at the same time. Breaking free of his grip, she ran stumbling through the snow. "Nicola! You're just in time."

Nicola stooped to embrace her, swinging the girl high into the air before letting her slide back to earth.

They came on together, Nicola's arm around Emily, Emily gazing adoringly up at Nicola.

She went to her aunt and uncle first, hugging them both before turning to Aidan with a quiet, "Hello." Her clear-eyed gaze had lost its shyness.

"Welcome home." Aidan kissed her, encountering warm lips and cold nose, a combination that had him grinning like a fool. The leap of his heart at seeing her confirmed the conclusion he'd skirted around days ago—

He loved her.

Good time to find out, he told himself sardonically, when you're scattering your late wife's ashes. Needles of guilt pricked him.

Then he looked at Nicola as she took in the urn, the setting and the people. The love and compassion in her eyes made him realize that, yes, this *was* the absolute right time to find out he could love again. And that the woman who'd brought him back to life, as it were, could only have been Nicola.

"We're each saying a few words and spreading a handful of ashes," he told her.

Nicola nodded. "I'm so glad I made it back in time."

Aidan offered the urn to June.

June, her nose red in the cold air, her blue eyes filled with tears, reached into the urn and took a handful of ashes in her brown kid leather glove.

She looked at her fist clenched around the gray granules. "My daughter," she said, choking on the words. "You were only human, but in my heart you will always be perfect."

Particles were already sifting free of June's fingers. She walked a few paces away and with a graceful arcing motion flung the ashes out over the mountain.

Roy took off his glove and plunged his bare hand into the urn, trying to scoop up as much of his daughter's remains as he could. He set the contents free in one swift sweep of his arm. "Charmaine," he said, his strong voice breaking. "You'll always be my little girl. Rest in peace."

Aidan held the urn out to Nicola. Her eyes filled with tears as she reached in and took a handful of ashes.

As she threw them wide, she said hoarsely, "Charmaine, you lit up our lives for too short a time. I was going to say goodbye but I know you'll always be with us."

Aidan held the urn down low for Emily. Her blue eyes, so like her mother's, were apprehensive. "Don't be afraid, honey," he said. "Your mommy wasn't afraid of anything."

Emily took a handful, spilling half of it back into the urn. "What do I say?"

"Whatever you want," Aidan told her. "Pretend you're talking to your mom. Say what you'd say to her if she were here right now."

Emily went very quiet, a look of concentration on her young face. "Mommy, I wish you could fly, up into the sky so you wouldn't fall."

Tears seeped from Aidan's eyes. "I believe she did fly in the end, Em. Right up into the sky."

Emily tossed her tiny share and watched it blow away, light as fairy dust.

Finally it was Aidan's turn.

He looked around, at his mother and father-in-law, at his daughter, at Nicola. Charmaine had brought all these people into his life. He felt the heavy urn in his arm, weighed down by the past. It was time to let Charmaine go.

Needing to be by himself, he walked past the others to the precipice and spoke low into the wind. "Charmaine, thank you for Emily. I will always love you. With your blessing, I will also love Nicola. For Emily's sake and for mine, I'm going to look to the future."

Bending his knees, he angled the urn and swept his arms in a wide arc, releasing the rest of the ashes. They caught on the wind and floated out over the cliff, to drift and settle over the mountain.

Charmaine was gone, but not gone. Aidan felt at peace.

CHAPTER FIFTEEN

"IT'S STILL SNOWING." Nicola let the drapes fall shut just as June's mantel clock chimed seven. The household had been subdued since the trip up the mountain this morning but in a good way, as if the ceremony had brought her cousin's family a serenity not attained at her funeral six years ago.

Sensing Aidan and Emily needed time alone Nicola had asked Aidan to call her later, then had gone back to June and Roy's. All through an early dinner she'd listened in vain for the phone to ring. Even if he called now she likely wouldn't see him tonight, not with all this snow.

She paced the room a couple of times, stepping around Grammy's slippered feet as she sat on the couch knitting.

"Why don't you call him, child?" she said, pulling on her yarn.

Nicola threw herself into a Queen Anne chair and twisted and turned, trying to get comfortable.

"It's Christmas Eve. He's probably busy with his family."

"You won't know until you try."

"Where's Aunt June?"

"Upstairs, I think."

Nicola trudged up to the second floor and along the passage. "Aunt June?"

"In here, dear," June said from Charmaine's room.

Nicola stood in the doorway, her eyes widening in surprise. June was seated at the vanity, wrapping Charmaine's hand mirror in tissue paper. At her feet was a large cardboard box half full of similar bundles. "What are you doing?"

June placed the package carefully in the box. "I'm just making a little more room for you."

"You don't have to do that." Nicola walked over and put an arm around her aunt. "Are you okay?"

"I'm fine." June smiled at her in the mirror. "The ceremony was lovely this morning, wasn't it? I think we all needed closure in one form or another."

Nicola hesitated. "Did Aidan show you the letter?"

June nodded. "He came over while you were gone and we had a long talk. Nothing can bring Charmaine back but I feel so much better *knowing* she wasn't trying to harm Emily." June's voice wobbled. "You can't imagine how that hurt me."

Nicola put her hand on her aunt's shoulder and squeezed. "Don't think about it anymore."

June drew in a deep breath and touched her eyes with a tissue. "Aidan's a nice man. I think our relationship will improve from now on." She gazed at Nicola speculatively. "He asked me if I'd mind if—"

"If what?" Nicola said.

"No, I won't preempt him." June picked up Charmaine's gold locket and held it out, the chain dangling over her hand. "Would you like to have this as a keepsake of Charmaine?"

"I would treasure it," Nicola said. "Are you sure?"

"Yes. It's a much more suitable gift than her dresses. I don't know what I was thinking." June shook her head at her own folly then smiled at Nicola. "I've always thought of you as a daughter."

"Thank you." Nicola hung the locket around her neck and bent to hug her aunt. "Thank you so much."

Grammy's voice came faintly up the stairwell. "Nic, your boyfriend's here."

Nicola cringed, embarrassed for Aidan to be referred to as her boyfriend in front of June. Especially considering nothing had been resolved between her and Aidan.

She took a deep breath and said to her aunt, "There's something I didn't tell you about Aidan and I…"

June smiled gently. "You didn't have to, dear. It's written all over your face when you look at him."

"Do…do you mind?"

"I think you're perfect for each other."

Nicola hugged her again then ran down the stairs, her heart beating fast. *Aidan hadn't called; he'd come.*

Grammy stood in the hall, trailing wool from the knitting in her hands. "Hurry up, those horses are stamping up the front yard."

"Horses!" Nicola rushed to the door. Aidan, looking years younger than he had just a week ago, had left a horse-drawn sleigh and driver at the edge of the snow-covered lawn and was coming up the front steps.

"Prince Charming has come to carry you away," Grammy chortled gleefully.

Nicola's chest was tight with excitement and happiness. To Aidan she said, "What's all this?"

"Christmas Eve is carol singing time in the Wilde family. I've come to take you to Tapley's."

"In a sleigh?" Nicola was already getting her jacket out of the hall closet. One arm in a sleeve, she paused and glanced down at her sweater and jeans. "Maybe I should change into something nicer."

Aidan dropped a kiss on her forehead. "No need on my account. I like you just as well in your bulky sweaters and blue jeans."

"You do?" she asked in surprise.

"Of course. Besides, you'll need to keep warm in the sleigh." He pulled a soft package wrapped in Christmas paper out of his jacket. "This is for you. An early present."

"Thank you." She tore the wrapping off. Inside was a soft cream-colored knitted scarf with matching hat and gloves. "Oh, they're beautiful."

"They're hand-knit by Liz from Fiona's alpaca wool."

"I love them." Nicola wound the scarf around her neck and put the hat on.

June came down the stairs. "Are you going out, Nic? Oh, good gracious!" she exclaimed, seeing the horses on her front lawn.

"Look what Aidan gave me, Aunt June," Nicola said, pulling on the gloves.

"They're lovely," June said. "Hello, Aidan."

"Hi, June. You, Roy and Grammy are all invited to come carol singing with us and to my parents' house for drinks afterward," Aidan said.

June fingered her string of pearls. "I don't know. We don't usually go out on Christmas Eve."

"There's a first time for everything," Grammy said, wrapping her yarn around her needles. "Count me in."

Roy appeared, glass of Scotch in hand. "What's going on?"

"Carol singing in Tapley's Estate," June explained. "The snow's too heavy to go out, don't you think? Aidan had to bring a sleigh to get here."

"I think the horse-drawn sleigh was more for romantic effect than transportation," Roy said, smiling at Aidan.

"The snowplow is on the highway, heading this way," Aidan said. "Another half an hour and your road should be clear." He smiled at Nicola. "That'll give us time to get back there."

Roy looked at June, who said, "Oh, why not. It'll be nice to see Leone and Jim again."

Out on the lawn, the horses stamped their shaggy hooves and snorted impatiently. Aidan grabbed Nicola's hand. "Your carriage awaits."

The sleigh creaked as Nicola climbed in. Aidan tucked warm blankets around them and nodded to the driver. With a jerk the sleigh pulled onto the snowy road and they set off, harness bells jingling.

At the bottom of Emerald Estate they crossed the highway to travel beside snow-covered Green Lake. The waning three-quarter moon had risen over the mountains, shedding silvery light over the open expanse. The runners on the sleigh made a shooshing sound on the snow and puffs of condensed breath came from the horses' nostrils.

Aidan took her hand beneath the blanket. "Why

did you come back? Was it for Charmaine's com-memoration?"

Nicola smiled up at him; he looked so handsome in the moonlight. "For that, yes. And for you." She squeezed his hand tighter, hoping he wouldn't notice the dampness of hers right through her gloves. "You asked if we could try again. I've decided I'd like to, very much."

Aidan's eyes grew dark as he bent his head and kissed her. Nicola was conscious of chill air on her cheeks and Aidan's warm mouth on hers...of the thudding of hooves...the pounding of her heart. Bells jingled. And the kiss went on and on....

The sleigh crossed the highway again at the River of Golden Dreams and continued down the Valley Trail with the river on their left and the sloping rise of Alpine Meadows Estate to their right.

Aidan glanced up at the lighted houses through the trees. "Nate and Angela's house is dark. They must already be down at Mom and Dad's."

"Is that where Emily is?"

Aidan nodded. "I dropped her off on my way to get you." He chuckled. "She wanted to come in the sleigh, too."

Nicola snuggled closer to Aidan. "You should have let her."

"Tonight is going to be packed with family," he

said, his dark eyes serious. "I wanted time alone with you."

"Oh?" Nicola held his gaze, her heart racing.

Aidan reached inside his jacket again and withdrew a small square package wrapped in gold foil. "Open it."

"You already gave me a Christmas present," she said, undoing the tape.

"This isn't for Christmas."

Nicola fumbled with the paper, uncovering a pale blue hinged box. Telling herself it was probably earrings or a necklace, she lifted the lid.

It was a ring—a small pear-shaped diamond set between emerald baguettes.

"Do you like it?" he asked. "Maybe I should have waited and we could have picked it out together but I…I wanted to show you how I felt."

She was speechless.

"Nicola?" he said anxiously, lifting her chin to search her face.

Tears filled Nicola's eyes. "It's beautiful. Exactly what I would have chosen." She blinked. "Is it…? Are you asking me…?"

"Take off your glove." Aidan removed his, too, and took the golden circle from her trembling hand to slip it over her ring finger. "Will you marry me?"

She felt the moisture in his palm. Unbelievable as it seemed, Aidan Wilde was nervous, too. "Are you sure?" she said, afraid his nerves were caused by doubts. "I wouldn't want you jumping into marriage because you're grateful to me or because you've been avoiding relationships so long you don't know what you really want in a wife."

"I don't need another second to know I want you," Aidan told her. "I loved Charmaine but ours was the blind passion of youth, without any thought given to sustaining a truly compatible relationship."

"We need passion, too, don't we?" Nicola said.

"We have it." He kissed the tip of her cold nose. "Don't you feel the chemistry between us?"

"I thought it was just me." Nicola nudged him in the ribs, teasing. "The night I arrived back in Whistler, when you came into Aunt June's living room, you looked right through me."

"You were doing your best to imitate a sofa cushion," he protested. "I admit, it took time for you to grow on me, but I was blocking emotional attachments."

"Can you love me as much as Charmaine? I don't want to always feel in my cousin's shadow."

"Believe me, Nic, you've come out from her shadow and the effect is blinding." Threading his fingers through her hair he pulled her closer and kissed her again thoroughly and very convincingly. "No more comparisons. Trust me, I know what I want, and I want you." He paused and looked at her. "Well? Will you?"

"Do you love me?" She had to hear the words.

Aidan grimaced. "I'm so out of practice I forget I need to actually say it." Again, his hand tightened on hers. "Nicola, I love you."

"I love you, too. And I will marry you. Should we ask Emily's blessing?"

"I already did. Her exact response was, I believe, *yippee*." Aidan smiled. "Now that you've accepted, I think she speaks for both of us."

Nicola twined her arms around his neck. "I'll remember this forever."

They heard the singing from a distance, a chorus of voices rising in the crystal night air. The driver drew the sleigh to a halt where the Valley Trail crossed the road below Tapley's and Aidan and Nicola got out. While the horses puffed and steamed in the chill air, Aidan paid the driver. Nicola kept touching and twisting her ring beneath her glove. Aidan loved her. The fairy tale had come true.

Aidan glanced at the gamine face beside him, unable to quite believe his good luck. He took her hand and they walked up the darkened road toward his parents' neighborhood.

They met up with the others on Balsam Way. June, Roy and Grammy were already there, part of the extended family group standing before an open doorway, singing to the people inside. Seeing them, Emily broke away from Leone to run to Aidan.

"Great-Uncle Roland's here!" she called excitedly. "I've got more cousins!"

"Roland, his second wife and their two teenage children flew in from New York today," Aidan told Nicola.

After smiling at everyone in greeting, Aidan and Nicola joined in the carol. His bass voice harmonized with her husky contralto and Emily's high-pitched lisp.

"'…peace on earth, goodwill toward men, that glorious song of old…'"

When they finished singing they were given eggnog and hot chocolate and stayed to chat a few minutes with the householders before moving on. With the festive decorations and the music, the atmosphere was similar to that of a street party, everyone stopping to exchange Christmas greetings.

Nicola's voice was hoarse and her head buzzing when they all trooped back to Jim and Leone's house. There was pleasant confusion in the foyer as boots were removed and coats hung up.

Roland's wife and children were feeling jet-lagged so they'd gone back to their hotel, but Roland had returned with the others to spend time with his

son. He was older than his brother Jim and his dark
blond hair was thick with gray, but he had the rugged
good looks of the Wilde men.

Jim built up the fire and Nate plugged in the
Christmas tree lights. Aidan got Roy a glass of
Scotch and made sure Grammy and June had seats
by the fire. Fiona insisted that Marc also sit down.
Rowdy, his Jack Russell terrier, immediately jumped
in his lap, certain of his welcome.

Nicola leaned against baby grand piano at the
edge of the group, soaking up the warmth and
laughter.

"Jim, if you handle the drinks, I'll get the food,"
Leone said. "Angela, Fiona, can you give me a hand?"

If she was going to be part of the family, she might
as well start now, Nicola thought. "May I help?"

"Of course," Leone said warmly. "Thank you."

Nicola was taking homemade mincemeat tarts
from a cookie tin and putting them on a plate when
she noticed the other women had fallen silent. Glancing up, she saw Angela, Fiona and Leone standing
on the other side of the counter, all staring at her ring.

"Is that what I think it is?" Leone asked hopefully.

Feeling herself blush, Nicola said, "Aidan gave
me this tonight. We're getting married."

"Hurray!" Angela cheered, quickly seconded by
Fiona.

"That boy! He never tells us anything." Leone came around the counter. "Give your future mother-in-law a hug."

Nicola hugged them all, several times over, amid much talking and laughing and even a few tears on Leone's part.

"It's never to early to start planning," Leone said. "What do you want for a wedding gift?"

"Stoneware," Nicola said promptly, sparking gales of knowing laughter.

In the living room, the female eruption of gaiety halted the men's discussion of which NHL teams would make it to the finals. Jim, Nate and Marc glanced down the hall toward the hullabaloo, then at each other.

"What do you think's going on?" Jim wondered.

Aidan exchanged glances with June who winked at him. "I'll go see," he said.

The moment he stepped foot in the kitchen he was bombarded with hugs and good wishes. Nicola stood back, grinning. He soon escaped with Nicola and the plate of mince tarts, followed by his mother and sisters-in-law. Jim, Roy, Nate and Marc were waiting expectantly while June and Grammy looked cautiously optimistic.

Aidan brought Nicola into the center of the room. "We have something to tell you all—"

"They're getting married!" Leone exclaimed, unable to contain herself.

The announcement required another round of hugging and congratulations. At last the excitement died down enough for everyone find a spot to sit and have something to eat and drink.

Glancing around the crowded room, Leone said, "Jim, you're going to have to build us a bigger house. This family has practically doubled in the past year."

Nate raised his glass and called for a toast. "To family. May the Wildes continue to expand and prosper."

When the cheers died down, Marc proposed a toast of his own. "To the healing power of love." He lifted his glass to his father then gazed into Fiona's eyes. "I, for one, have been blessed."

Quieter but no less heartfelt murmurs of "hear, hear" greeted Marc's sentiments.

Jim raised his glass to his brother Roland. "To father and son being reunited." Then he tipped his glass in June and Roy's direction. "To families reunited by marriage. And to Nicola," he said with a warm smile. "Welcome to the family."

Aidan reached for Nicola's hand and smiled around the room at his parents, his uncle, his brother and cousin, their wives, Nicola and her aunt, uncle and grandmother. Last but not least, his daughter, who'd been playing with the dogs and ignoring all the adult talk. Now she sensed his gaze on her and smiled at him. His heart was full.

"This has been a big year for all of us," Aidan said. "It's been full of positive changes which have given us hope for even better times to come." He raised his glass one final time and met Nicola's loving gaze. "To Christmas—past, present and most of all—future."

CHRISTMAS MORNING Aidan got up first to light the fire and to make sure Emily's stocking was full and that all the presents were under the tree. With the kindling crackling and the tree lights twinkling, he stepped back to contemplate the recent changes in his life.

Charmaine's dust-collecting pieces of crystal were gone, but her urn still sat on one end of the mantelpiece balanced by three carved wooden elephants Emily had lost her heart to and June had indulgently bought her as an early Christmas present. Oh, well, Aidan thought, there are worse sins than being too giving.

He glanced up at Charmaine's portrait. Thanks to Nicola he no longer felt haunted by her image or guilty at her memory. He hoped Charmaine would have approved of him marrying Nicola and been glad for them. On the whole, he thought she would.

Charmaine, for all her self-indulgence, had had a generous spirit.

"I'll take good care of our baby," he said, renewing his promise to her. "Nicola will not only love Emily as if she was her own, she'll love her because she was your daughter."

He turned at the quiet tap of slippers on the hardwood floor. Nicola stood there in her new silk velvet dressing gown, one of many presents he'd showered her with. "You're up early."

"I was too excited to sleep." She came to stand beside him and twine her arms through his. "I feel like a kid again. Do you think we should wake up Emily?"

"I *am* awake." Emily ran into the room and stopped short, staring at the tree with wide eyes and open mouth. When she'd gone to bed last night only a handful of presents for other people had been under there. Now it was piled to the bottom boughs with brightly wrapped gifts.

The next hour was full of laughter and excitement as each present was unwrapped and exclaimed over. All three of them sat under the tree amid the discarded paper and ribbon and thoughtfully chosen gifts. Aidan had had to disappoint Emily in the matter of a puppy, but promised her one next summer when better weather would make house-training a dog easier.

"You haven't opened this one," Nicola said, handing Aidan a large flat package.

"You've already given me too much," he said, glancing at the pile of books, CDs and the sweater she'd given him. Nevertheless, he tore open the wrapping with anticipation.

"Do you like it?" she asked.

Aidan nodded, his heart too full to speak. Nicola had had the photograph of herself, Aidan and Emily in front of the Christmas tree blown up and framed. "I love it," he said at last then met her gaze. "I love you. We'll make a special place above the mantelpiece for this."

"That's all the presents," Emily declared. "We've opened every one."

"There's one more for you, Emily," Aidan tore a big red bow off a piece of wrapping paper and pressed it onto the top of Nicola's head, laughing at her surprised expression. "I got you what you wanted most."

"A mom for Christmas!" Emily shouted. "Thank you, Daddy. Thank you, Nicola." She threw herself at each in turn and hugged them hard.

"I got what *I* wanted most," Nicola said to Aidan, her eyes shining. "You and Emily."

"And I have a family," Aidan said with quiet satisfaction. "Peace of mind and love in my heart."

Emily jumped up, showering them all with ribbon and bits of wrapping. "This is the best Christmas ever!"

HARLEQUIN *Super*ROMANCE®

A six-book series from Harlequin Superromance.

Six female cops battling crime and corruption on the streets of Houston. Together they can fight the blue wall of silence. But divided, will they fall?

Coming in December 2004,
The Witness by Linda Style
(Harlequin Superromance #1243)

She had vowed never to return to Houston's crime-riddled east end. But Detective Crista Santiago's promotion to the Chicano Squad put her right back in the violence of the barrio. Overcoming demons from her past, and with somebody in the department who wants her gone, she must race the clock to find out who shot Alex Del Rio's daughter.

Coming in January 2005,
Her Little Secret by Anna Adams
(Harlequin Superromance #1248)

Abby Carlton was willing to give up her career for Thomas Riley, but then she realized she'd always come second to his duty to his country. She went home and rejoined the police force, aware that her pursuit of love had left a black mark on her file. Now Thomas is back, needing help only she can give.

Also in the series:
The Partner by Kay David (#1230, October 2004)
The Children's Cop by Sherry Lewis (#1237, November 2004)

And watch for:
She Walks the Line by Roz Denny Fox (#1254, February 2005)
A Mother's Vow by K.N. Casper (#1260, March 2005)

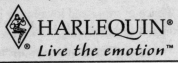

HARLEQUIN®
Live the emotion™

www.eHarlequin.com   HSRWOMIB1204

HARLEQUIN® *Super*ROMANCE®

YOU, ME & THE KIDS

Along Came Zoe
by Janice Macdonald

Superromance #1244

On sale December 2004

Zoe McCann doesn't like doctors. They let people
die while they're off playing golf. Actually, she knows
that's not true, but her anger helps relieve some of
the pain she feels at the death of her best friend's
daughter. Then she confronts Dr. Phillip Barry—the
neurosurgeon who wasn't available when Jenny was
brought to the E.R.—and learns that doctors
don't have all the answers. Even where
their own children are concerned.

Available wherever Harlequin books are sold.

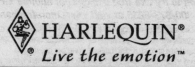

HARLEQUIN®
℗ *Live the emotion*™

www.eHarlequin.com

HSRYMK1204

If you enjoyed what you just read,
then we've got an offer you can't resist!

Take 2 bestselling love stories FREE!

Plus get a FREE surprise gift!

Clip this page and mail it to Harlequin Reader Service®

IN U.S.A.
3010 Walden Ave.
P.O. Box 1867
Buffalo, N.Y. 14240-1867

IN CANADA
P.O. Box 609
Fort Erie, Ontario
L2A 5X3

YES! Please send me 2 free Harlequin Superromance® novels and my free surprise gift. After receiving them, if I don't wish to receive anymore, I can return the shipping statement marked cancel. If I don't cancel, I will receive 6 brand-new novels every month, before they're available in stores. In the U.S.A., bill me at the bargain price of $4.69 plus 25¢ shipping and handling per book and applicable sales tax, if any*. In Canada, bill me at the bargain price of $5.24 plus 25¢ shipping and handling per book and applicable taxes**. That's the complete price, and a savings of at least 10% off the cover prices—what a great deal! I understand that accepting the 2 free books and gift places me under no obligation ever to buy any books. I can always return a shipment and cancel at any time. Even if I never buy another book from Harlequin, the 2 free books and gift are mine to keep forever.

135 HDN DZ7W
336 HDN DZ7X

Name	(PLEASE PRINT)	
Address	Apt.#	
City	State/Prov.	Zip/Postal Code

Not valid to current Harlequin Superromance® subscribers.

Want to try two free books from another series?
Call 1-800-873-8635 or visit www.morefreebooks.com.

* Terms and prices subject to change without notice. Sales tax applicable in N.Y.
** Canadian residents will be charged applicable provincial taxes and GST.
All orders subject to approval. Offer limited to one per household.
® are registered trademarks owned and used by the trademark owner and or its licensee.

SUP04R   ©2004 Harlequin Enterprises Limited

eHARLEQUIN.com

The Ultimate Destination for Women's Fiction

For **FREE online reading,** visit
www.eHarlequin.com now and enjoy:

Online Reads
Read **Daily** and **Weekly** chapters from
our Internet-exclusive stories by your
favorite authors.

Interactive Novels
Cast your vote to help decide how these
stories unfold…then stay tuned!

Quick Reads
For shorter romantic reads, try our
collection of Poems, Toasts, & More!

Online Read Library
Miss one of our online reads?
Come here to catch up!

Reading Groups
Discuss, share and rave with other
community members!

For great reading online,
visit www.eHarlequin.com today!

INTONL04R

HARLEQUIN®

AMERICAN Romance®

Baby to be

A Baby to Be is always something special!

SANTA BABY
by Laura Marie Altom
(November 2004)

Christmas Eve. Alaska. A small-plane crash—
and nine months later, a baby. But Whitney and
her pilot, Colby, are completely at odds about
their son's future. Until the next Christmas!

THE BABY'S BODYGUARD
by Jacqueline Diamond
(December 2004)

Security expert Jack Arnett and his wife, Casey,
are getting divorced because she wants children
and he doesn't. But—and Jack doesn't know this—
Casey's already pregnant with his child....

www.eHarlequin.com   HARBTB1204

Visit Dundee, Idaho, with bestselling author

brenda novak

A Home of Her Own

Her mother always said if you couldn't be rich, you'd better be Lucky!

When Lucky was ten, her mother, Red—the town hooker—married Morris Caldwell, a wealthy and much older man.

Mike Hill, his grandson, feels that Red and her kids alienated Morris from his family. Even the old man's Victorian mansion, on the property next to Mike's ranch, went to Lucky rather than his grandchildren.

Now Lucky's back, which means Mike has a new neighbor. One he doesn't want to like…

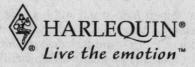

HARLEQUIN®
Live the emotion™

www.eHarlequin.com

HSRH001204